Lost Enough

A collection of short stories

Anita Dolman

MORNING RAIN PUBLISHING

Lost Enough

By

Anita Dolman

Copyright 2017 by Anita Dolman

Cover & Book design 2017 by Morning Rain Publishing

Digital ISBN: 978-1-928133-82-7

Print ISBN: 978-1-928133-83-4

Published in Canada

This book is a work of fiction.

Names, characters, places and incidents are products of the author's imagination or are used fictitiously. Any resemblance to actual events or locales or persons, living or dead, is entirely coincidental.

Publication History

"Terrarium," *Matrix Magazine*, Summer 2016, Issue 105, Montreal.

"Pacific Standard," *Triangulation: Lost Voices* anthology, Parsec Ink, 2015, Pittsburgh.

"Handcrafting," *On Spec: the Canadian magazine of the fantastic*, #97, vol. 26, no. 5, summer 2014, Edmonton.

"Happy Enough," *Morning Rain Publishing*, February 13, 2014, Burlington; and in "Romantic Shorts" e-anthology, *Morning Rain Publishing*, February 14, 2014, Burlington.

"Bureau," honourable mention, 6th Annual Geist Literal Literary Postcard Story Contest, published on www.geist.com, spring 2010; and in *Peter F. Yacht Club #16: VERSeFest special!*, February 2012, Ottawa.

"Sunday Brunch," *The Storyteller Magazine*, Vol. 15, Issue 2, April/May/June 2010, Maynard, Arkansas.

"Starting," *Peter F. Yacht Club*, No. 12, fall 2008, Ottawa.

"Alumni magazine, classified ad," *Geist*, No. 51, winter 2003, Vancouver; and published as "Dear Classmates: An alumni note" in *Utne*, No. 123, May-June 2004, Minneapolis.

Resources

"Blackfoot Legend", Head-Smashed-In Buffalo Jump, 1987, Fort Macleod, Alberta.

Acknowledgements

Thank you to everyone who encouraged me in the writing and revision of these stories. Particular thanks go to James K. Moran, Sarah Tsiang, and Dominik Parisien for their editorial guidance, and to Fabienne Glauser, rob mclennan, Steven M. Blois, Jackie Stanford, Amanda Earl, Vivian Vavassis, Michael Adams, Amanda Robertson, Courteney Lawrie, Elizabeth Dolman, Yolande Dolman, Janice Lescarbeault Moran, Ken Moran, and my parents, John and Ietje Dolman, for all of their various and ongoing support over the years.

Additional thanks to Rhonda Douglas, Roger Delisle, Michael V. Smith, Julia Gualtieri, and the late John Lavery for their brilliant insights and excellent advice at different stages in this project, and to Jennifer Bogart and the rest of the Morning Rain Publishing team for their expertise and patience and, most of all, for believing in this book.

Thank you to the Head-Smashed-In Buffalo Jump world heritage site in southern Alberta for the use of the quote at the start of "Starting." I would also like to acknowledge that the land on which I live, and on which much of this manuscript was written, is the traditional unceded territory of the Algonquin Anishnaabeg people. Much of this manuscript was also drafted on land that is Treaty 7 territory and the traditional territory of the Piikani Nation (Blackfoot).

Stories from this manuscript have appeared in *Matrix Magazine*, *Triangulation: Lost Voices*, On Spec: the Canadian magazine of the fantastic, *Geist*, *Peter F. Yacht Club*, *The Storyteller Magazine*, and *Utne*.

Anita Dolman gratefully acknowledges the financial support of the City of Ottawa.

This book is dedicated to James, for believing in me, and to Ietje, for giving me two languages and a love for all of them.

Contents

Handcrafting

Sylvia pours two mugs of green tea and returns the silver teapot to its tray on the Airstream's wooden counter. Like the teapot, the high edges of the wooden tray are decorated in a shallow relief of fine, ornate patterns likely to be missed by any new friends who might come to visit Sylvia in her kitchen. She hears a diesel truck come down the hill into the campground. A rust-mottled pick-up grinds past. The harsh smell of fuel wafts into Sylvia's world, overwhelming the earthy scent of hot tea.

"We have new neighbours, I think," she calls to George. Her words roll out in heavily accented English. It still feels odd to Sylvia, speaking this new language with George after so many years in another shared tongue. They are both trying their best to assimilate, to take in this new country in every way possible, so that it can be theirs, too.

George naps every afternoon while Sylvia knits shawls and baby clothes for her children and her grandchildren. Sylvia walks the length of the camper, to the rear bedroom, to bring George his tea. She sits on the edge of the bed.

"You did hear the truck?" she asks, carefully laying out her grammar. "I said 'I think we have neighbours.'"

George rolls over to look at his wife. His right shoulder, exposed by the fall of the blankets, is thick with grey hair. Sarah smiles inwardly. She has begun picking up second-hand paperbacks from the sale racks by the doors to the small town grocery stores where they shop. She reads them in the evenings, keeping a dictionary on her lap. Last week, she learned the word *hirsute*. Like a suit of hair. Not like George. George's hair is too

9

unruly to be a suit, she thinks—too *pig-headed*, like him. She has learned this phrase recently, too, and pictures George lying in bed, an enormous pig's head on his shoulders, great tusks jutting upwards. The image is not entirely unbecoming and reminds her of festivals held when she was younger and very far away from this campground in northern British Columbia.

"You see who they is?" he asks.

"Who they are," she corrects him.

"Are, then." He takes the mug of tea from Sylvia. "Did you see them?"

"No. Just their truck. They have a camper on top—a *fifth wheel*. Old. Not clean and new."

"Old is okay," says George, sitting up with his tea. "We are old, too, and we are okay."

"Speak for yourself," says Sylvia. "I am okay, but I am still young."

"Young like the Earth is young." He laughs, then grows serious. He leans toward her with affection. "And so beautiful like the Earth, too."

She responds with a soft murmur in their native language.

There is a burst of rock and roll music from outside, the slam of a truck door, perhaps three or four campsites away, around the bend in the lane.

After dinner, George builds a fire in the fire pit. The days are shorter already, the evenings cooler. Sylvia brings out a shawl for herself and a blanket for George. She folds the coverings over the backs of their lawn chairs. She goes back inside to get her dictionary and her book, and the wind-up lantern.

Returning down the little steps, she says, "I do not know why you look with that thing."

George is setting up his telescope, as he does every evening at dusk. The tripod has stretched its feet into the soil or sand of hundreds of campgrounds. This time, he has set it up on the grass-sheathed knoll behind their site, and Sylvia must look up toward the forest above in order to talk with him.

"I look in, I do not recognize a thing," she says.

"It is the best that money can buy," explains George again, adjusting the eyepiece. "It shows what is there. You cannot expect things to stay the same."

"Maybe things would not look so different if you did not drop it so much."

George grumbles in their former language.

"English, George."

"Bah," he answers.

Together, the two notice the sound of approaching footfalls on the gravel lane. With one last look toward George, Sylvia settles herself down in her chair. She drapes the shawl across her shoulders and rests the heavy dictionary on her legs. She opens her book.

"You should read this book, George. The author, he is write about... he is *writing* about different way world could have been, with castles still and zombies and wars. It is silly. You would like it."

"Castles and war is different?"

"Castles and war like in old times, but with zombies— and dragons."

"What are *zombies*?"

"Hi," says a quiet voice. A young woman has come around the front of the trailer and is standing a few steps down the wide lane of George and Sylvia's campsite. She clears her throat. She looks like she is glued in place on the gravel, unable to move any closer. Her shorts are so tiny that at first Sylvia is not certain the girl is wearing anything other than her sandals and a dirty, hooded sweater.

"Hello," say George and Sylvia together after a pause.

"Looks like yous are the only other campers here, so I thought I'd come by and say 'Hello,'" says the girl.

Sylvia can see that she is nervous.

"My name's Mabel," she continues, rocking forward on one foot and quickly back again, as if remembering she has not yet been invited into George and Sylvia's outdoor living room.

Sylvia appreciates the gesture of respect.

"I am Sylvia." She slides her bookmark back into place before closing the book, but keeps her thumb between the pages as well, in case the visitor does not stay long. "The man dreaming of the stars is my husband, George."

"Very nice to meet you both," says Mabel. "My husband... gosh, that seems so weird to say; we's only been married a couple days... we stopped in Prince George last night, and we's here for a few days before we do the coast. Rick, that's his name, he wants me to ask if yous would have some catsup. I guess I forgot to get some, and he likes it on his KD. He's particular that way, I guess."

"Catsup?" asks Sylvia.

"Tomato catsup."

The young woman is clearly from an English-speaking place, but Sylvia has not heard her style of speech before.

"Some folks say *ketchup*," says Mabel.

"Ah! Yes, ketchup. But no, no I do not think we... Wait. It comes in those little packets, yes? At the restaurants where food is fast?"

"That's it," says Mabel, hope brightening her sallow, acne'd face.

To Sylvia, she looks unwashed. It is difficult to imagine this ragged child as a beaming bride only two days before. Sylvia notices the faded red sweatshirt is not as loose at the belly as it might be.

"I will go check," she says. "You come in."

In the tight space of the kitchen, the young woman's smell makes it clear she has not bathed since the wedding, and possibly not for some time before. Sylvia breathes through her mouth as best she can while looking in the little refrigerator for the packets she has collected, not wanting to waste food, but also not wanting to consume the plastic-wrapped red and yellow pastes.

"Where are you and your husband from?" asks Mabel. She moves out of Sylvia's way by pressing herself along the checkered bench by the dinette table. Sylvia joins her, taking a seat on the opposite bench.

Sylvia is in no hurry to get the packets. She wishes to know more about the girl and how she came to such a situation in this modern world, with its many preventions and rights. "Oh, we are from very far. Our grandchildren, though, they have emigrated all over the world. Some to this Canada. It is a beautiful land, this. I have several granddaughters here expecting babies. You are how far to go now?"

Mabel's eyes grow wide. "You can tell?"

"I am sorry," says Sylvia. "I was indelicate. I am an old lady. I have seen very much birth. Very much death, too, but very much birth. Beginnings are good. You are young, though, for a Canadian. For a modern girl. You are how old? If I can ask you this?"

"I'm seventeen."

Mabel looks unsure of the age she has given, and Sylvia wonders if perhaps the girl is even younger. "That is very young. But good. You will have much energy for your little one." Sylvia closes her shawl across her chest.

"I guess," says Mabel, even more uncertainly.

Her hands are folded in her lap like a schoolgirl's. Sylvia thinks the girl looks very worried. In the clearer light of the hanging lamp, Sylvia can see the shadow of a bruise beneath Mabel's left eye.

"Do you have a lot of kids?" asks Mabel, her gaze still fixed on her own hands. "I guess you must have, if you have a bunch of grandkids."

"I had many children, once," says Sylvia. "And now I have a great many grandchildren. Lately there come more and more new babies in our family. We are very fortunate, George and I. May I touch your stomach? I have a sense about these things."

Mabel looks up. Her eyes look frightened, but she nods and moves to the edge of the bench so the old woman can reach across to her small belly.

Sylvia can feel that the girl must be nearly four months along.

"A boy," says Sylvia. "Very strong. Very healthy."

"You can tell that, just by feeling?"

"My people have always had this gift," explains Sylvia. She slides her hand underneath the bottom elastic of the soft sweater and spreads her fingers wide across the girl's stomach. She fixes her eyes on Mabel's and says firmly, but quietly, "He will not be like his father—do not worry."

The two sit still for a full minute. Sylvia continues to gently massage Mabel's stomach all the while. The girl, quieter and calmer than before, breathes slowly and deeply in time with Sylvia's touch.

"I should go," says Mabel at last, as if waking up. Sylvia draws her hand back from under the sweater and Mabel stands to leave.

"The catsup," Sylvia reminds her.

"Oh, right. Thanks."

Sylvia finds the plastic packets in the fridge and gives these, along with a container of organic stew, to Mabel.

"For the baby's strength," she says. Mabel nods her thanks.

Outside, at the bottom of the little steps, Mabel turns back to Sylvia. "I like your shawl," she says.

"I will knit you one if you like," says Sylvia from the doorway. She gives the girl a grandmotherly smile to let her know she would gladly do this for her, and, she hopes the girl understands, much more as well. "They are quick to make."

"Oh, you don't have to do that," says Mabel, looking up at the old woman. She looks toward where her husband and their truck must be, beyond Sylvia and George's trailer. "Plus, we're only here another night or two."

"We as well," says Sylvia. "Now, promise me you will not be eating any of those junk foods yourself. That sort of thing is not healthy for a baby. You must take good care of yourself and your baby for me. Such unhealthy things are only for that young husband of yours. You understand? You promise you eat this for dinner tonight instead, okay?"

"Okay," says Mabel, backing away the first few steps. "I will. And thanks."

Sylvia watches the girl go out of view.

"I do not like it when you do that," says George after the girl is well away. Sylvia can see he is as compelled as ever to make his point one more time, even though he must know these words will have no effect on her. "There is no advantage there. We should be picking only the very best. These ones, the girls, you just pick them because you feel sorry. You are... *bleeding heart.*"

"There must always be variety," chides Sylvia. "You know that, George. We cannot pick them all one type and only hope it works out."

George is done with his telescope for the evening, and is dismantling the pieces into their large, metal case.

"We do our best only if we keep the diversity. How else they survive? I cannot tell what they might need later any more than you. We just give them their leaps forward each time when they are ready. That is all I can do." Sylvia has settled back into her chair, her book and dictionary resting on her lap. Instead of reading, though, she folds her arms across her chest. On the one hand, she is tired of having the same argument over and over again with George. Yet, something comes alive in her each time they have this discussion. She sits still, listening to George meticulously unscrew, polish and lay down each piece of the fancy equipment.

"And yes," she starts again after several minutes, "my heart bleeds for poor little person machines like that. They do not make up so many of our grandchildren as they used to, but there are still too many of them, and if I can do for them, I will. Their men will not help them, so then there is me."

"Is that our job? To help the ones who would not make it otherwise?"

"It is our calling to give all of them, the whole humanity, a future, George. We are their caretakers. Their grandmother and their grandfather. That is us."

George opens the door to the trailer and takes the heavy case inside. The door drifts and clicks closed behind him. It opens again a moment later.

"Once we were their *gods*," says George, the screen door drifting closed again as he comes to the fire. He takes his seat next to Sylvia, spreads the patchwork blanket over his legs. "Now we are their *scientific advancement*. I read, too, you know. In the newspaper. *Geneticist*. That is what they would call you. No altars, no goats. And they think they can do it themselves. Pretty soon, they will not be needing us at all. They will decide to have seven arms and breathe soda pop and grow tails again. And become *zombies*."

"Yes. A *geneticist*. I have heard that word, too. But I like it. Their geneticists, though, they just study and play with the thises and the thats and the pieces."

"Next town, I will buy you a laboratory coat. You can look the part."

"It is not our part, George. We do not *study* the genetics. We are their genetics."

"You say this, but it is true they make their own genetics now. We will be out of business soon. You will see." George is pointing his finger at Sylvia for emphasis. She knows the gesture is meant to infuriate her.

"Hah!" snorts Sylvia. It is a strong sound, coming out deep and resonating in the trees above. Sylvia softens her voice. "They do not know what they are doing, what is needed," she says. "We do this since the time of the valleys. We are their survival. They have prayed to us, brought us offerings. We have given them many futures."

"And now we are giving them *catsup*," finishes George. A teasing smile plays in his eyes.

"Hmmph," she says, but a grin starts to creep across her lips as well. The frustration has passed.

George reaches his hand out to hold Sylvia's, and they sit watching the fire together until another log crumbles red and smouldering into the ash.

"We need to leave tomorrow," says Sylvia, cautiously. Her small hand is warm inside of George's larger one. Her gaze goes back up into the forest, then to the stars. "I help her a little bit more than with the leaping of the baby."

George grunts another ancient word through clenched teeth and pulls his hand abruptly away, out of her reach. Sylvia sighs. She knew George would be upset, but she could not resist.

"He is no good to her," says Sylvia to the woods. "He could having hurt the baby," she finishes, turning to George. Her eyes are pleading. His face is softer, more forgiving than she had expected, but she continues as though he has argued the point with her again. "You destroyed an entire army before our last sleep," she says. "You cannot get so angry when I finish one stupid little man."

"I am not angry you want him finished," George says, pulling his blanket up around him. "I just think you should mind your own work. I am not *obsolete* yet."

"You are not obsolete, George," says Sylvia. "You are *natural selection*. They still write about you, too. They know more about you than about me."

"I know what the bearded scientist called me." George pouts toward the fire, then reaches over for a log to add. "One of these days," he says, "I go call the stupid little science magazines, and I explain. I show them what their Darwin and their Mendel did not understand. What they still not understand, with their equipment and their ideas."

George prods a new log into place in the heart of the fire, jabs the pieces of disintegrated log beneath into charcoal dust.

"George?"

"Yes?"

"I think after we make this leap for them, I would like to watch. Do you think we could, instead of having to sleep again? I think it is an important time, this time. We should stay. In case they need us sooner."

George puts the poker back on the earth beside his chair and takes Sylvia's hand. He lets out a deep and thoughtful sigh.

"You know if they make a great destruction, there is nothing we can do for them then," he says. His voice is soft. In its tenderness, Sylvia hears for the first time that he has become as concerned as she has been since they woke and saw this new world their grandchildren had made.

"I know," she says. "It would be so lonely again for so long, though, if they end it. I want to give them everything we can, George. They are so much like real grandchildren. My heart, like you say, it does very much bleed for them."

"Okay, then. This time, we will stay."

"Thank you, George." Sylvia settles back into her chair and listens to the sounds of the night woods around them, the scuttle of timid animals into their homes, the burble of a small creek beyond the knoll, the quiet closing of the day's flowers. She catches the scent of distant factories and machines pushing more chemicals into the forest air from many miles away.

"Would you like me to make some more tea?" she asks.

"Yes," says George. "I think that would be good."

Day One

Sophie Grant

Let's say this is the day my life changed. It hasn't. Not yet. But let's say it is. That way, there is a clear date on which my life changed.

When, someday, someone asks, "When did your life change?" Which they might; you never know; it really depends on the kind of change. I can say, "It changed September 6, 2011." Because look, I've written it down. It's official. There it is.

And any minute, it will.

The thing that is whatever is coming will come. Will be here. Will be happening. Will have happened.

I should help it. These things don't happen on their own. I should do something. I'll go online. I'll buy... No, that's silly. No one's life changes from buying anything. Even I know that. I'll call... who? Anyone who could have changed my life is ancient or dead. Or is no longer answering my calls. Or, more likely, has never heard of me. What important person would know a 39-year-old waitress with nothing to show for any of it but a stack of past-due notices, a three-year chip, and a grown son who can't bother to remember her birthday? Although, that's more my fault than his.

Shit. Stop that. This is supposed to be a time of change. Today is the day I learn... I meet... I see...

Fuck it. I'm going for a walk.

Christopher Bruge

This is stupid. Somebody just shoot me.

"Ma'am... ma'am, I've been trying to get bus fare all morning to see my girlfriend in the south end. You wouldn't have any spare change or a bus ticket or anything would you? I really need to get to see her. She's not doing so good."

She might, she might. She's not young enough to think this is a come-on. Not so old she'll tell me to get a job. Nice brooch, though. You don't see those much anymore. Especially on a woman who looks like she's lived a pretty jewel-less life. What the hell am I thinking?

"No, sorry, I don't carry change."

Dammit.

"Okay, thanks anyway." Shit, shit. Buck 12. Useless, fucking useless. Goddam people. Nothing. I can't get anything for this.

"Sir... sir, I've been trying to get bus fare all morning to see my girlfriend in the east end. You wouldn't have any spare change or... " Holy fuck! He's stopping!

"Sure. Hold on."

He's digging. A toonie. And a loonie. Yes! Never should have underestimated. Jake says suits never stop for beggars, but he's wrong. Hah! He'll love that. If he can still love anything. If he can still think. Please let him still recognize me.

"Thank you! Thank you so much. You really don't know what this means to me." And here comes the bus. I'll be damned! Thank you, god, thank you.

Alycia Sachedina

Gardenias might be good. All those little blossoms bundled together into big puffs of white. And not ostentatious. Dad's already angry about the bills, about having to pay for anything for his daughter. If Mom were still alive it would have been different. But at least he's agreed to it.

If it happens.

Why does everyone on the bus always smell like wet dog, even when it's beaming out? This guy doesn't even look like he's bathed in a week. Don't sit next to me, don't...

"Excuse me, may I...?"

"Of course."

Must be gel. He doesn't smell bad at all. Who would look like that on purpose?

What is wrong with people? Why did he step out into the street like that last night? It wasn't my fault. It wasn't. They don't have enough lights on Cardwell. It's a thoroughfare and they don't even have working streetlights most blocks.

Maybe hurricane lamps on the tables. They're low enough so people could still see each other, plus they're romantic. Hurricane lamps and gardenias. Understated. Everything an about-to-be-convicted bride could want.

Stop it. There is no way they can link me to him. There was absolutely no one else around. I looked. I remember looking. And I braked. I was braking. I didn't hit him full force. He could still be okay. It was only, like, a footnote on the news. Everything could still be okay.

Elisa Arnold

This is not my responsibility. It is not my fault my sister works in emergency. I can't help that I'm the one she called when she recognized him as my friend.

Plus, I've done all I can. I gave them his boyfriend's number. I'm sure he's on his way by now. I've done the right thing. If I stayed, I would only make it worse.

Ninety-three guys. Five girls. This is my life's accomplishment: a list of lovers who leave the next morning. This one may die because of me. Even if he makes it, he's going to feel like he betrayed his boyfriend. I know he will. That's why he ran out. Whatever idiot hit him probably never saw him coming.

"Oh, sorry." Jesus, I can't even leave properly.

"Hey, watch where you're going! You crushed my new pump! What is wrong with you?"

"Hey, do you know this is a hospital? For all you know, I could have just lost someone! Be a person, already."

Fine, spin around and head right back out. Not like anything else is sane today. Hey, is that a *Wedding Belles* sticking out of her purse? Miss Minty-Fresh has found love, and I'm starting to kill off my one-night stands?

I'm really sorry, Jake, but I need to go. I'll think good thoughts for you. I promise.

James Zeitveld

Brother? Boyfriend? The driver? He can hover by the vending machines, but I'm certain he's here for this room. If he's still here in ten, I'm calling security. Poor guy in there has enough problems.

The next hit and run that comes in, I'm quitting my nursing degree and giving up on humanity. No, that's not fair. There are lots of good people. Like Sophie. I hope she likes her party tonight. It will be nice to get to know her better. You'd think you'd be surrounded by the most caring people at a hospital, but you can't beat Sophie for a good word for all. If it weren't for her taking my shifts at the diner every time the hospital schedule changes, I'd have lost my job here by now.

"Hi. My name is James. I'm just here to check on you. Hope you don't mind the talking, but there's growing evidence you folks can hear what's going on." IV's fine, catheter doesn't need emptying. "I know. The ventilator's a lot of noise. I think they do that just to make it more dramatic."

"Hey, look. They figured out your name, and they've called someone. Plus, you made it through the night. As signs go, that's a good one."

"So, what do you say? You need anything?" Poor guy. "Bet I can guess. Would you like me to? Guess I'm going to have to take silence as consent here. "

"Just wait here. I'll go get him."

Jacan Lang

I hear him breathing. It sounds like when we're talking in the night. Normal. Close. I'm glad he's come closer. *Why can't I wake up?*

I'd give anything to tell him how sorry I am. For what's happened, for the argument, for what I did, for the accident. This stupid, stupid accident.

He's proposing. Proposing that he'll propose if I wake up.

Wake up. Tell him that he's an ass. Tell him you love him. Tell him yes.

That must be the doctor. They're being too quiet to hear. They don't sound positive, though: "... yes... fiancé... damage... have to... and wait.... ventilator... his wishes... next of kin..."

Next of kin would be my Mom, I guess. I don't even know where she lives, so I don't know how anyone else is going to find her. Was there a return address on that letter she sent last month? I never even checked. First letter in years. Why didn't I check? She said she's three years sober, getting her life back on track. I hope she does. I hope she... Shit, I could die, couldn't I?

I don't want to. I just got proposed to! I'm not ready. I want to get married by the fountain in Laurier Park. I want to see my Mom again.

Christopher and Jacan

Say something.

"You wouldn't believe what I went through to get here." Moron. What a thing to say. What if he can hear you?

"I mean Elisa's sister—you remember Tory? We met her at Elisa's show. She works emergency and recognized you. Your ID was gone, and she couldn't remember your name, so she called Elisa, who called me. But I thought it was you, and I was still angry about what you said, but it kept ringing, and I thought it's our first real argument in over a year together, and I can see how maybe I was kind of in the wrong for making out with big, dumb, and handsome, but it didn't mean anything, and I think maybe I did it to be sure how much I meant to you, and yes that's really dumb. But it was Elisa, and then I had no money, and this guy in a suit gave me change for the bus, and I thought you'd think that was funny, and I really need you to live."

"Elisa says the cops are trying to track down your mom, but you've never said much about her. "

"Jake, I need you to know I don't care what you were doing on Cardwell Avenue at 3 a.m. I know who lives there, so I can guess. But, if you make it through this, the minute you wake up, I'm going to propose to you. I promise. I just need you to wake up."

James and Sophie

"Happy birthday, Sophie! Sorry to leave you sitting in the parking lot so long. I just wanted to check on a patient one last time."

"That's alright. Get on in."

"It's great to finally see you away from the diner. You have to let me make the wait up to you, though."

"You don't have to do that, honey. It's more than enough that you're getting me out to celebrate. Anyway, it gave me a chance to people watch. It's amazing what you see outside a hospital, especially when people don't know you're watching."

"Creepy."

"Not at all. Well, maybe sometimes. See the girl on the bench? She's been picking the petals off an entire bouquet of gardenias, one at a time. I don't know if her guy loves her or not, but I feel bad for the gardenias. Who's your special patient?"

"Young guy. Hit and run. The doctors have no idea yet if he'll make it. I left him with his boyfriend, who was too afraid to even go in at first."

"Lord. And here I've been feeling sorry for myself today."

"What for? You're about to go to your birthday party, which you will love. Nice broach, by the way."

"Thank you. It was my grandmother's. I've had this feeling all day like something important was going to happen, so I thought I'd dress for it. I even wrote in my journal this is the day my life will change. I guess I thought... Well, I wrote my son a letter last month, trying to make amends, and I thought maybe Jacan would try to contact me today. But nothing so far."

"Sophie?"

"Yeah?"

"What did you say your son's name was?"

Overgrowth

From far back in the ditch, Jules hears a rustle in the marsh grass, spots a dark movement among the sun-spliced strokes of green. She sprints toward a broad maple, ducks behind, surveys the land around her.

A knight steers his black horse out from the cover of the lea, past the bobbing stocks of dried cattails, onto the dirt lane. Jules scans for the overgrown walkway leading to the castle gate. The sound of hooves pounds faster against her heart as she rushes for the entrance. She holds her flowing skirts high as she leaps over the tangles of weeds and sprawling dogwoods, which menace her ruined rose gardens. She hears the malicious snort of the stallion as it rears, the knight's savage roar. She dives shoulder-first across the threshold, into the shadows beyond the castle door.

Safe, Jules turns to see the groundhog bounce away behind the rusty dogwoods.

Inside the empty, wooden house it is calm and dark and cool—a quiet refuge from the August heat and the oppressive continual buzz of cicadas and power lines. In her tumble, Jules scraped her arm along the torn linoleum of the forgotten kitchen. She sits cross-legged inside the empty doorway, inspecting her jacket. Twin streaks of grey dirt stretch from the shoulder to just above the elbow. She brushes against it back and forth, with the palm of her hand. Nothing is torn. Lucky. Foolish to play such a childish game, even if no one was looking. She's fifteen. Far too old to pretend anything anymore. She looks the kilometre down the laneway toward the concession road. It is too far away and too blocked by summer's high grasses and overgrown seedlings to see, except where the tiny gap of dusty laneway allows the rare flash of a car kicking up dust and gravel. She listens as a killdeer tweets at her, still hysterical over Jules' wild dodge past its nest.

"My children, my children! Look how you've frightened my children in their eggs!" Jules imagines the frantic mother screeching. She wonders if killdeer are naturally nervous because they make their nests on roadways, or if they build their nests in the road because they want a reason to be upset all the time.

"No offense," says Jules to the bird. "But I know some people like that, so, you know... It seems like a fair question."

Jules stands and dusts the dirt from her jeans. Once upon a time, she and Carrie would ask their moms for cleaning supplies and load their bike baskets full of paper towels and Windex and garbage bags to make something of the house. Once, Carrie biked the entire way from her house while balancing a broom along the length of her bike, the straw head perched on the handlebars, the wooden shaft bouncing on her thigh with each turn as she pedaled behind Jules. The girls had dreams that they would clean and fix the house until it was real.

"Remember that? We figured we could make you a contender," says Jules in the direction of the iron mass that was once a working wood stove. "Once."

"Not likely," answers the house. "I was always destined for the fields."

"You and me both," answers Jules, to which the house has no reply.

Jules steps carefully around the ever-expanding hole in the kitchen floor. There is more rustling, this time stemming from the exposed pile of wood and plaster that blankets the earthen basement below.

"At least you're still good for something," she says, peering down. "Looks like you have new tenants."

"Aren't you just full of delightful observations and self-pity today? Stop by anytime if you want to act like this. I don't get enough misery out here anymore. Be careful, by the way. I think they're skunks."

The hole has crumbled open so wide that the only way for Jules to take the last step to the staircase is to swing around the chasm by grabbing the newel post at the base of the stairs.

Great, she thinks to herself in mid-leap. *I could die stinking.* The thought strikes her as absurdly funny, and she lands smiling. *Or I could just stinking die.*

That thought isn't funny at all. The darkness of the house, so cool and welcoming minutes before, shoots through her and chills her suddenly from the inside out.

"House?" she calls, starting up the stairs.

"Jules?" The house mimics her.

"Don't leave me, please, house."

"Never, Julianna. I promise."

What remains of the top layer of wallpaper has hardened in time to a dry, yellow gloss stretched along the walls from scrape to hollow. Within the deepest fissures, at the frayed edges of boot-kicked holes and natural disintegrations, Jules can see the exposed strata of decades of other papers beneath. The bottom layer—a plaster of newspapers from the time the house was built—is Jules' favourite thing about the farmhouse and has been since she and Carrie first stole inside at the age of nine. New friends on a Sunday bike ride to Belmore for ice cream, they had stopped and dared each other to get closer, then closer, and then to go in. For Jules, the house is her first, and, so far, her only, love, although she now abandons it for months at a time, visiting, when she does, mostly on her own, to think through the things she can't deal with anywhere else.

From the top landing, Jules steps gingerly down the hall, from board to remaining, withered board. After each step, she pauses to make sure she has firm purchase. The only planks still to be trusted are those centred on the joists, so she waits to confirm the solid feel of a two-by-four beneath her sneaker before launching as lightly as she can to the next remaining surface.

The master bedroom is still mostly intact except for its far corner where an ancient maple has grown relentlessly into the house becoming a part of the building. The wide trunk has pushed through the walls and deep inside the room. Its branches have forced the window frames out of their casings with glacial slowness and strength. When Jules first came here with Carrie, the tree—still outside, but with its roots already grinding through the shallow foundation far below—had only nudged its outline against the south wall. A handful of twigs rapped patiently against the broken glass of the window.

Lately, in this room, Jules gets the sense that the entire structure has become a treehouse. The thought makes the room, and her, feel weightless, attached to nothing, not her life, not the ground. She pictures herself and the branch-wrapped building floating away across fallow fields.

"Don't laugh," says the house. "This will happen to you, too, someday."

Jules understands what she means.

"Not me," she says. "I want to be cremated."

"Same thing," says the house.

"Faster," says Jules.

"Yes. Faster," answers the house.

A pale rectangle in the middle of the floor marks where a rug must have once sprawled beneath the bed. The bed frame, its corroded springs lolling from the slightest movement in the room, has been hoisted onto its side against one wall. Jules asked Carrie to help her do this last fall, so that she would have more room for her project.

Jules goes to the closet and slides two fingers through the dark circle where a doorknob would once have been. She tugs deftly. Inside is a whole other time.

"What is it you're always looking for in those newspapers?" asks the house.

"I thought you knew everything," answers Jules.

"I know a lot. And I know very little. What is it you're hoping to find in there? A different life? A different you?"

"Maybe. Yeah. Another me. Where I'm shilling 1956's latest mink fashions. Or making the perfect roast duck for my husband and our two-point-four white-bread children."

"If you mock them, why do you read about them so much?"

"Mind your own business, house."

Jules' mom, Genevieve—Jeanie—and her husband, Mike, will be coming home from the airport tonight. It's a six-hour flight from Paris. That, plus customs and the time needed to pick up their bags and then the two-hour drive from the city means that Mike's brother, Rob, won't get them home until at least eight o'clock. Jules unhooks her pocket watch from the coin pocket on her jeans. She listens to the second hand tick its way around the top of a minute, then unclicks the silver lid to look inside. The watch was her inheritance from her real father's father. It says it is just past six o'clock.

It has been ten days since Jules' mom and Mike left for France. Jeanie's father died of a stroke in his hometown in some southern province Jules can never remember the name of. Jeanie and Mike booked tickets as soon as they got the call. Jules' mom said they had to go, because he was her father, no matter how horribly he had treated her, and they had to do what they could for the funeral. Jules assumed right away that they were only going to see what they would get from the will, or what they could snatch from the old man's house before other relatives showed up. They left Rob in charge of the farm and sent Jules down the road to stay with Carrie and her family.

Jules' French grandfather didn't have much money, from what Jules has gathered, so she imagines her Mom is by now reeling from disappointment that there was no secret stash. Jules can't speak French and only met the old man the one time he came to visit the farm, so she never had a chance to ask him about his life. Instead, she only has her mother's untrustworthy accounts of stinginess and cruelty.

Jules' own father, she recalls, hated the man, although she can't remember why. She can picture her dad once telling someone that his father-in-law was a real bastard. Through the dreamy haze that cloaks all her memories of her father, Jules also thinks she remembers him telling her she should never trust her grand-père if she had the choice. With "the bastard's" death, though, the last of the men Jules was ever related to is gone.

Jules had not considered this before, had only thought about the old man's death as a thing unto itself. Now that she is in the safety of her house, of her room, she realizes this final death has left her truly alone with her Mom in the life her Mom has created.

Still cradling a stack of stained newspapers in her arms, Jules plunks herself down under the weight of this new thought, settling both herself and the stack onto a carpet of dust and dried leaves.

Swallowing a shudder of mournful solitude, she pushes her thoughts toward her papers instead. She starts to lay them out around her in small stacks, by month. Today's pile is 1948 to 1950. These ones were not wallpaper, although she does have samples of those in another pile. Today's papers were insulation in the attic.

The first time, two years ago, Mike slipped into her bedroom in the dark while his wife lay asleep in their room down the hall. Jules' Mom had passed out after a night partying with her friends. It had been someone's birthday. Jules woke up with Mike's hand covering her mouth, his hot breath on her face.

"She'll never believe you," he whispered. "Only me."

Jules knew he was right. And she never told anyone. Until Carrie, last night.

At first the rage Jules felt was not directed at Mike, but at herself. How could she never have thought he would do the same to Carrie? Why did she never tell Carrie, so, at least, she would be forewarned? But Carrie hadn't known, couldn't have known. She only knew that Jules no longer wanted to hang out as much, and that she wasn't as much fun anymore when they did get together. During the moonlit conversation in Carrie's room last night, Carrie told Jules that she had put the differences in Jules down to high school, to new friends, to diverging interests. And so Carrie, not knowing, got into Mike's car when he offered her a ride the last week of school.

Today, Jules' anger is all for Mike.

On page seven of the October 29, 1949, *Star*, a boy and girl, eyes disconcertingly wide open, sit at a checkered table in excited awe of their mother, who is displaying a loaf of bread for the camera. Their mother is proud and perfectly groomed, her tiny waist tied up in apron strings. To Jules, the whole family looks like they have been painstakingly moulded out of hard, pink candy.

"House?" she calls out. "I have a question."

"Fire away," says the house.

"You're old."

"Be nice, Jules."

"No, for real. You've been around a long time, I mean."

"I remember when that tree first sprouted."

"So you've seen a lot of people."

"A long time ago I housed whole families. People came for parties. There was a wedding in the yard, once. A big affair. They roasted a fat pig and danced until morning."

"Were any of those people like this?" Jules points to the family, their toaster gleaming in the background, their collars starched pertly, their happy, happy faces mugging for the camera in exacerbated triumph over war and poverty and all the other memories still nipping at the kitchen door in 1949.

"No," says the house. "Not a one."

"Do you think they existed anywhere? People like this?"

"I'm just a house, Jules. Things exist for me or they don't. You need to understand that for people it's different."

"Why?"

"Because people can dream."

Jules stares at the family in the picture for a long time, then at the next image, and the next until the shadows grow too deep within the room for her to make out the words on the pages. Held up to catch the fading light from outside, the slender, metal hands of her pocket watch tell her it's 7:30. She folds the newspaper shut and goes to the window. Looking past the thatch of branches, she can see the fields out beyond the overgrown yard. She gathers up one of her stacks of papers and heads to the door. Turning back, she scans the darkening room one last time. The house is being reclaimed more each year by the trees and the animals and the moss. The roof won't survive another winter. Jules thinks of all the times she has sat in the middle of this room, looking for something that she has always known never existed, but for which she has always longed nonetheless.

Jules retraces her stepping stone route through the hall and back down the stairs. Pausing on the bottom riser, she uncoils the elastic from her ponytail and twines it around her bundle of newspapers. With a solid throw, she tosses the package over the hole in the floor, to the safety of the front door. She tugs at the newel post again with both hands to test that it is still solid, then swings herself over the dark maw below, to the strip of floor remaining at the far edge of the hole. She teeters too far forward on her toes and quickly corrects, forcing herself back against the wall to regain her balance. Several somethings scratch and titter below as Jules inches carefully toward the swath of mottled green linoleum by the door.

On solid footing again, she opens the hall closet. Inside is the broom, an old towel, a box of Kleenexes, and the ancient, glass paraffin lantern. She pulls the lantern from the shelf and swings it back and forth to check that there is still plenty of liquid sloshing in the chamber. She closes the closet door and picks up her papers. From the threshold, she looks back toward the stove. To her, the white, iron hulk—rusted and inaccessible across the hollow floor—has always seemed like the house's heart.

"Don't say it," says the house.

"But—"

"It's okay," says the house. "We both know that I know."

Jules feels a wash of love for the house, and for everything it has given her.

"Go on," says the house.

"Thank you," whispers Jules.

She has left it until too late in the evening. The bramble-charged lane that skirts the nearest field is difficult to see in the dimming light. She follows the double ruts of the homemade truck lane as they continue into the narrow woods behind. The oaks and maples, holding hands high above, are already blocking out the last of the sunset. Twice, Jules nearly falls with the lantern; once going all the way down on one knee.

As Jules emerges from the woods, a thin strip of sky still blazes orange above the forest at the other end of Mike and Rob's secret field. Jules wades though the tall corn planted by the men to hide their crop. She sets her lamp down on the ground and shimmies the elastic off over the end of her paper bundle. Jules was relieved when Carrie said she didn't want to go to the police either. Neither of them wanted to tell their story to a room full of cops, or to a judge who would decide if he feels like believing them.

Jules lifts the glass chimney from the top of the lantern, then turns the tiny screws holding the metal cap to the base. The thick, withered cloth of the wick is dry, and she casts it aside among the plants. She dips sheet after sheet of old newspaper into the kerosene, making a row of wetted paper flutes. She carries the first flute far away and lights it with one of Mike's lighters. She holds it to the leaves of one of the marijuana plants as if it is a candle, but the green leaves only smolder at first. She gathers another cone and lights it, this time laying it in the arms of a nearby corn stalk. She watches the fire bloom almost instantly and races to get more of the flutes.

By the time Jules throws the sixth flute, the fire has caught well enough that she can go. She flings the lantern, and the rest of her stack of newspapers, further into the field before backing away toward the trail in the woods. She remembers the lighter, pulls it from her pocket and launches it far into the fire, too. She checks her hands and jeans quickly for obvious evidence. Although she doubts it will be the arsonist the police care most about arresting. If they do bother to investigate, Carrie and her mother will swear Jules has been with them the entire time. Like family.

Jules watches the spreading blaze for one more moment before she starts to trot, then run, toward the lane. She stumbles briefly now and again in the rutted darkness, but stays on her feet the entire way through the trees, then past the open field.

The moon and the stars are glowing vibrant above as she gets to the backyard. Jules stops to catch her breath. She can see the tree's branches have already begun to push through the shingles, exposing the first line of rafters to the sky. Jules and the house say nothing to each other before Jules turns and runs the secret path to Carrie's farm.

Momentum

The sound of a dog, of several dogs, folds through her. Far away. A basic sound. Harsh. There's something else, too— something she can't describe. There's a gun in the backseat. No, she's not thinking clearly. But there is, she remembers it, a gun in the backseat. The fog feels like it's lifting, then it blossoms around her again, renewed, constricting, like... not like fog. Like a drug. She must have been hit over the head— that's how they got her in the car. And there is a gun, but it's in someone's hand. A man's. In the backseat. And she's in the front, but she can't see clearly, not yet. What language are they speaking?

Harold is driving. The magnolias are in bloom the air is fresh and clear, tossing the occasional gust of blossoms into their path like petals at a wedding. It's Sunday. There is a picnic basket in the back seat, and Harold is smiling at her. For a moment, she thinks he looks sad. He has been working hard at the store, and with the wedding coming up he must be so tired, but he's strong and always manages a hopeful, boyish smile. He makes her feel good, feel cared for, no matter what. She has the sudden sense that everything is going to be okay—can feel it in the warmth of the sun on her arm, the smoothness of her skirt beneath her fingers. She reaches out, touches his cheek, feels the line of his smooth-shaven jaw, and everything is okay.

German. There is a war going on. She sees lights ahead, a bridge, a blockade. Everything else around them is dark, although she knows there are towns here. She still can't see clearly. They've noticed she is awake, but she is tied, her wrists bound to a piece of metal in the dash. They're laughing. A joke at her expense. The man in the back seat runs his gun along her face, presses it between her breasts, pulling her blouse forward with the tip, looks down her shirt, says they're little but they'll do, for Jew tits. More laughter. She spits at him. She can't help herself. She knows she should play along, that it would be safer, but she can't help herself. She will not be debased on her way out. She has lost enough already.

The road is winding. Harold's sister has made them chicken sandwiches, and they're driving up to the orchards for a picnic. She spins the engagement ring slowly around her finger. It's been four months since Harold proposed at La Maise. She cried. So did he. Both of them so full of excitement and relief. The wedding will be in the fall. Harold could come live with her in her parents' house. They could fix it up. Harold is handy; he could reshingle the roof and replace the plumbing. She could finally decorate, finally fill it with life again. She can see the river below as they crest the hill. It shines bright blue in the sunlight dancing between the rocks and trees of the valley.

Blackness again and then a sharp light that wakes her. She is lying on smashed concrete, in a giant puddle of water and God knows what else. Everything hurts. Everything between her legs feels shredded and brutally sharp, but she cannot cry any more tears. She feels empty and hateful. Another line of men forms in front of her from the door. The next is unzipping his pants and climbing on top of her. Laughter is bouncing off the walls. She wants to die. She wants to kill them all. She wishes she could gather all the pain around her and explode it like a bomb, take them all with her. She screams through the gag, and they laugh louder.

The blanket arcs in the air and settles on the grass with a whisper. Harold sets up the rest of their lunch, plates and napkins, wine glasses, a bottle of champagne. He has insisted on doing it all himself, since she's always the one cooking for him. She takes off her shoes and feels the grass sliding between her toes. She wanders away a bit, up an aisle of apple trees, as Harold finishes his setting up. There are songbirds twittering back and forth everywhere from behind the leaves. She looks back toward Harold, sees him set out a small pot of yellow flowers.

Her clothes have been gone for what feels like days, but with little light, it is impossible to tell how long it has been since they brought her here. They've started bringing her just enough food—a bit of water, wet bread, and a yellowish soup—so that she doesn't lose consciousness. And there are gaps of hours now, maybe even longer, between the groups of men. Sometimes just the leader of the men who brought her here comes in. He says in heavily accented English that he needs to make "certain you still work" before he uses her himself and leaves. She tries to be somewhere else each time. This is just my body, she says, they can't get to me. I'm not really here. No one is dead, and I'm not really here.

There is no more putting it off. They are done lunch, and she has already had two glasses of champagne. She feels her heart beat faster, and a feeling of momentum, of racing down a hill. She has known Harold for over a year, but she does not know how he will react. He already pictures their life a certain way. She starts to tell him about how she was born in Germany, during the Great War, how her parents brought her to America as soon as it was over. And then she says it.

"Harold, they left me a house. I hear it's not in good shape, but I think we could fix it up. You're so good with tools, and my uncle says he could get you a job at his company. What would you think of moving back to Germany with me?"

Pacific Standard

The rain brings calm. It dims the hospice's rooms and settles the souls within them.

Claire sets the TV in Mr. Lui's room to the soap opera none of his family knows he has secretly followed for 23 years.

"Claire! You are like sunshine beaming into my day," says Mr. Lui.

"Thank you, Mr. Lui," answers Claire. "It's always a pleasure to see you, too."

Mr. Lui is one of Claire's favourite patients. His gratitude always welcomes her into the room like a hug. During his first week and a half at the hospice, at two minutes before 2 p.m. each weekday, Mr. Lui would pull out his breathing tube and try, with a voiceless, straining whistle of sound, to lift his head and speak.

Felipe, the nursing assistant on duty, had tied Mr. Lui's wrists down to the bed in the soft cuffs used to restrain the obstinate and the demented. Claire was in the next room that day, changing an IV for Mr. Walkley. She heard a scuffle as the young man tied Mr. Lui down, heard him tell the old man to stop and lie still, heard him mutter "old fool." Claire counted to five. Inhaled. Exhaled. Told herself not to do it. Then she walked in and went straight to the TV, turning it on, and setting it straight to Mr. Lui's channel. When she turned back, she saw Mr. Lui lying on the pillow, looking to the screen. His toothless smile circled the tube leading down to his throat and reflected tenderly in his watery eyes. He nodded weakly to Claire before fixing on his story of family politics and corporate subterfuge.

"It was creepy," Claire later overheard Felipe say to a small gaggle of nurses and staff gathered at the rear nurses' station. "Like she knew just what he wanted. She just came right in and turned the TV to a soap, and he calmed right down."

Since that afternoon, Claire has been careful not to get caught responding so obviously to any of her voiceless patients. One day, though, she knows she will. Already, she can't resist visiting Mr. Lui everyday to tell him about the world, or to answer his questions.

"No, not yet, Mr. Lui," she says today. "Yes, I promise I'll let you know." She has closed the door behind her, but cannot keep it shut for long without raising suspicion. "Yes, he said they would be coming later today. No, you know I can't tell him what you're thinking. I could suggest it myself, though, if you want. I could say it's what a lot of people in your state like. Does he know which kind is your favourite?"

All of the hospice room windows have a view, either of the mountains or the bay. Patients who can still talk and appear aware seem to care far less about the view than the ones who can no longer speak. Of course, when the only activity left to a person is harbour-gazing or the tracking of snow's movements as it accumulates or melts on distant, crumpled rock, the view takes on much greater meaning. Patients no longer able to see or speak, along with those mute with pain or sorrow, and those officially labelled vegetative, seem to care the most of all. They all ask what their view is, and Claire tells them. Sometimes she lies if it is not what they want, and there is no one to correct her.

Patrick, at 23, was the youngest of the hospice's patients when he arrived. He had wanted a view of the mountains, even if he couldn't see them. He told Claire the ocean was too enormous to contemplate in one lifetime, let alone in one as short as his. Plus, he had wanted to face the mountains where he had snowboarded. So, Claire asked Mrs. Laidlaw, who said she did not care about views, to please demand the room across the hall. This way, the floor manager would automatically trade her and Patrick.

A boating accident had led to Patrick's head injury, and to a chain of internal damage that was slowly causing his organs to shut down one after the other. He had been in a coma for more than a year and had been moved to the hospice because the end had become inevitable and was approaching quickly. Even if they thought Patrick might not know where he was, his parents and sister wanted him to finish his short life somewhere kinder and more peaceful than in the hospital where he had spent the past year.

Patrick caught on faster and with less surprise than anyone to what Claire could do. She had come into his room at the start of her shift to check on the new patient.

"Hello," she said.

"Hello," he answered in his head. To Claire, the instant response was like an electric shock. It thrust her back several steps. She fumbled, then quickly regained the saline bag she was carrying. It was as if had expected her to hear him. She asked him later if he had tried answering that way with everyone who had talked to him in the past year. He admitted he had.

"The relief when you answered back, all surprised, with your 'Oh. Hey! How'd you know about me?' was the best feeling I'd had since before the accident," he told her.

From "Hello," their conversation wound and rambled on into the days and weeks that followed.

After Claire had him transferred across the hall, Patrick asked her to describe each one of the mountains she could see. The next day, he asked for the edge of the city—how it looked at night, and then in the day. At his promptings, she described the row of semidetached houses and low apartment buildings across the street, the market on the corner, the street itself, its parking spots, the coming and going of people, the wooden benches and magnolia trees in the parkette below.

Patrick's stillness was newly disconcerting each time Claire talked with him. He was young and blond and handsome and still looked strong and vibrant, despite having spent over a year in bed. Even knowing better, she always had to fight the feeling that Patrick might wake up at any moment. To see him lying there, eyes closed, as peaceful as if asleep, it looked like there was no reason he wouldn't get up soon, get himself dressed, and head out to go snowboarding or sailing.

Somewhere between the mountains and the parkette, he asked Claire what she looked like. She gave him her height and her hair colour. Then he asked her to look in the mirror instead.

"Tell me exactly what you see," he said.

Hesitantly, carefully, she described the shade of her eyebrows, the colour of her lipstick, the freckle in front of her right ear.

Claire began to take most of her breaks in Patrick's room. She read him the paper, stayed late to read him the latest book by his favourite author. At home, she researched the answers to things he said he had always wondered about, before the accident, but had thought he would have time to find out later: The differences between crocodiles and alligators. How many kinds of spiders there are. Where the world's highest road is and to what altitude it climbs. What the coloured parts of a fruitcake are made of. What rank his grandfather held during the war.

Mostly, though, he wanted to know about Claire. He would ask her about her life, where she grew up, what she liked, what she had cooked for dinner the night before. He wanted to know what she thought of political issues, whether she felt the environment could still be saved, and what she would do to help other people if she could. To the last, she answered she was already doing what she could think to do. Patrick considered this for a long time, but did not answer.

No one—not her patients, her past boyfriends, or her family—had ever been so interested in who Claire was and what went on in her mind. Not since her mother died when Claire was six had she felt so listened to as she did with Patrick.

Claire knew she had to start being more careful about being seen going into Patrick's room. She stopped visiting quite so often, and, when she did, she timed it so no one would spot her unless she was heading in as part of her rounds. The incident with Mr. Lui's television was still to come, but the other staff clearly had already started to think of Claire as strange, and the amount of time she was spending with a coma patient, no matter how cute, couldn't be helping.

Claire mentioned to Debbie, a senior nurse, that she had heard coma patients could understand more than people thought they could.

"Just don't forget that we have twenty-four patients here at any time, Claire," answered Debbie. "And they all deserve just as much attention."

Still, Patrick's presence pulled Claire toward his room when she walked by.

One day, Claire had placed Patrick's hand on the page of the hardcover book she was reading him so he could feel the paper. Her shift was over. The door was closed. She lifted the book to turn the page.

"Stop!" he called.

The burst of sound in her mind, surely louder than he had intended, startled her, and she dropped the book to the floor.

"Sorry," said Patrick as Claire retrieved the novel from under the bed.

"That's okay," she whispered. She wished once again that patients could hear her the way she heard them, so no one passing in the hall would be able to hear her end of the conversation.

"No. No, it's not," he said. "I wanted something, but I don't have the right to ask it."

Claire listened closely to hear what it was, but there was only silence from Patrick.

"What is it?"

More silence.

"I wanted to feel your hand," he said.

Claire sat back down at the edge of the bed. She folded her hand inside Patrick's. For a long time, they sat like that. Then Patrick said "Thank you, Claire."

She looked at the sleeping features of his face and wished they would come alive, just once, when he spoke.

"Patrick, I've been wondering: what colour are your eyes? You're wearing sunglasses in the picture by your bed."

"Hazel," he answered.

Mr. Lui has a pregnant granddaughter. She and her husband visit Sundays, from one to two p.m., before one of Mr. Lui's sons and daughters-in-law. When Claire comes in for her Monday shift, she sees the granddaughter has pinned an ultrasound picture on the cork board in Mr. Lui's room.

The fetus must be roughly six months. Claire stares at the white tracery of a human shape for several minutes before checking Mr. Lui's chart.

"Can you hear what everyone thinks, or just some people?" Patrick asked.

"Everyone. Usually," Claire answered. It was her weekend off, and she had come in to see him. "I can't always hear you, though. Sometimes I get the idea you're able to block me from seeing or hearing certain things."

"So it works, then," he said. "I wasn't sure."

"How do you do it?"

"Practice. I've been a vegetable about sixteen months now. Not much to do but play with your own thoughts. At least, there wasn't until you came along. Say, I want to talk to you about something."

"Sure. What is it?"

"Every morning I hear Miss Featherston ask you if it's today. At first, I thought she'd just gone off her rocker, but the way I never hear your answer makes me wonder."

Claire watched the rise and fall of the blanket over Patrick's chest.

"Please don't ask, Patrick."

"You can tell when people who are dying will die, can't you?"

"No."

"No, as in you can't tell, or as in you're not going to tell me?"

"No, as in I can tell when *everyone* is going to die."

She had never told anyone that. Not that there were many people left in her life whom she could, or would want to, talk to about such things. It becomes more, rather than less, difficult knowing people's inner truths all the time. There can be good reasons for a person to lie. Or, at least, to skip over the finer details.

"You mean if you're standing in line at the grocery store, you know when the check-out girl is going to die?"

"Uh-huh."

"Your mailman?"

"August fourteen, 2027. At eight nineteen p.m."

"Kids?"

That morning in the parkette below, two black-haired sisters played with a bright yellow dump truck, driving loads of fallen magnolia blossoms from one end of a bench to the other, then dumping their pink haul over the edge. One will grow old, and the other will die of an aneurism at the age of twenty-seven.

"Yes," said Claire.

"What about babies?"

For the first time, Claire deeply regretted visiting Patrick.

"Babies are harder," she answered. "I can't read their minds, exactly, since they don't have words. But, I can usually sense what they want before their parents react. They don't shout their expiration date, though, the way older kids or adults do. Sometimes I get it anyway, but not usually. I've thought a lot about why. I like to think that most of them are like an unwritten book. Anything is still possible. The plot hasn't been mapped out yet."

Claire was looking away from Patrick, her gaze fixed on the grid pattern of the curtains. She did not want to hear his date in her head again.

"Claire," said Patrick.

"Yes, Patrick."

"Promise me something, please. Promise me you won't tell me mine, even if I ask."

"You're pregnant," says Mrs. Beasley.

"How did you know?" Claire is taken aback. Tomorrow, she has a meeting with her supervisor. She will have to give her maternity leave notice and hope for the best. She is already four months along.

"Dear, look at you. Anyone with eyes can see," says Mrs. Beasley, clapping her hands together in joy. The old woman has been growing physically weaker, but is still communicative and feisty, in her faded English accent. Some patients come into their own away from the families to which they have been beholden for so long. They feel they can be themselves at last, without anyone to whom they need to be accountable.

"I would guess you're about four months along, now," says Mrs. Beasley. "Assuming this is your first, of course."

"It is."

"Are you happy?" she asks.

The dying always cut to the chase, thinks Claire.

"I am," she says, unwinding the blood pressure band from Mrs. Beasley's arm.

"Claire?" asks Mrs. Beasley.

Claire looks her in the eye. The old woman's eyes are more glassy than when she arrived, but they still shimmer a soft green. Claire likes Mrs. Beasley the best of any of her older patients, and the feeling has seemed mutual from the start. Claire feels Mrs. Beasley gets something about her that

Claire can't explain, or doesn't want to explain, to anyone else. Something that has nothing to do with her special skills, but instead with her as a person.

Mrs. Beasley clasps Claire's arm suddenly but gently.

"Be happy," she says.

Claire feels the knobs of the old woman's arthritic fingers wrap dryly around Claire's thin wrist.

"Be happy," the elderly woman says again. Claire sees great earnestness now in her gentle eyes. "It goes so fast. Be happy every chance you get, okay?"

Claire plans to work right up until the baby is born. Her supervisor signs the papers to take Claire off heavy lifting duties and offers her congratulations. Claire can tell the woman, who is not much older than her, wants to ask about the father. But it is not her legal right to ask, so she doesn't.

"It was an ex-boyfriend," offers Claire. "He's not in the picture anymore." Tears unexpectedly well behind her eyes. She keeps them back, forces an awkward smile. "But it's a good thing," she continues, her voice holding steady over a canyon of emotion. "I'm happy. I'm a good age for it. And, of course, I have a good job that I really like. I think we're going to be fine."

"I'm absolutely sure of it," lies her supervisor.

During Patrick's last month, Claire became all the more careful about visiting him. One night, rather than leave after her shift, she hid in his bathroom until Beverly, the nurse on duty, came around to shut off the room lights.

"I wish I could kiss you back," said Patrick as Claire pulled away.

"Me too," Claire whispered. She had decided to be honest with him, as much as she could—far more honest than she had been with any of her previous boyfriends, at least. It was only fair.

"Claire," he started. He seemed to love saying her name, started most sentences with it. "Do you ever want to have kids?"

Claire's head rested on Patrick's chest. Beverly had come by only twenty minutes ago and would not be back to check up on the patients for at least another hour.

"Did you?" she asked Patrick.

"That is not an answer," he teased. Then, "I always thought I would be a dad someday. I was only twenty-two when this happened, so I thought there would be plenty of time. You know—in that someday, way off future. To do the grown-up part of life, I mean. Fall in love. Buy a home. Have a boy. And a girl. And a cat."

"Who would be giving birth to the cat?"

"Funny."

Not for the first time, Claire pictured Patrick walking, talking, holding her hand in the park. She also pictured a little boy, or maybe a girl. Running around. Playing, laughing.

"I used to want to have kids," she said after a long silence. "I used to think I could do it. Have a relationship like other people. But I don't think so anymore."

A wordless wave of sadness swept over her from Patrick.

"I've tried," she said. "But to hear everything someone is thinking—it's not right. People need to process their new thoughts and their feelings before they show them to anyone. And some should never be shared at all, truth or not. But I hear it all fresh. And it's awful sometimes. You can't look someone in the eye if you know what they really just thought about the woman you're passing on the sidewalk, or about what you're wearing, or that you left a stupid spoon on the counter or... anyway, I don't think I could try it again. Not with anyone else."

Claire, still lying next to Patrick, propped herself up on her elbow.

"I know this is going to sound ridiculous," she said. "And, just to be clear, I'm not downplaying what you've gone through, or all of your losses. But, Patrick, I think you're the perfect man for me. And you'll probably be the last."

From Patrick's mind came an image of him crying.

Claire is seven months along, and Mrs. Beasley is hanging in against all odds, although another stroke has taken most of her speech.

"No hiding it anymore, is there?" she says to Claire.

"No, ma'am," Claire whispers with a smile. Her bump has grown round and high and stretches the pink, patterned fabric of her uniform even when she is standing completely still. She feels like she is growing a beach ball.

"Are you ready yet?" asks Mrs. Beasley.

"Oh, almost. You should try to speak out loud, though, for practice, Mrs. B."

Mrs. Beasley ignores her.

"Do you know if it's a boy or a girl?" she continues. "Not that it matters these days, I suppose."

"It's a boy."

"Oh, congratulations! Do you have a name yet?"

"Yes. Patrick."

Mrs. Beasley winces in pain as Claire rolls her onto her side to change the sheets beneath her.

"Claire, dear, I know it's none of my business, and you can tell me just where to go with my questions if you like. But, where is the father now?"

"It's okay, Mrs. B. I trust you. His father was a patient here. A young one. He died six months ago—before you came."

"Oh, my. Did he know? Oh, I'm sorry. That was rude. I didn't mean to ask that."

"I know, Mrs. B. Hold on. I have to roll you the other way."

The older woman helps turn herself as best she can, to keep Claire from straining too hard.

"Yes, he knew," Claire answers after a moment. "He wanted it this way."

"And you, dear? What did you want?"

The old woman is settled onto her new, white sheets. Claire loosely folds the old ones and slips them into the hamper trolley waiting by the door. She considers her answer, pictures Patrick. Not in his bed, but in the photo his sister had placed by his bed. Patrick on a gleaming, white motor boat. Smiling in the summer sun. Bare-chested, in Bermuda shorts and sunglasses. One arm around his equally blonde sister, another toasting the cameraman with a beer.

"The same thing as him, Mrs. B," she says. "The same thing as him."

"Oh, my poor girl."

Claire told Patrick she had missed her period by several days. She had gone to the store to buy a pregnancy test, but the instructions all said she would have to wait at least another week before she could take them.

"That's okay," said Patrick. "I don't need a test. I just know. I know we're going to have a baby."

"Me, too, Patrick. I know it."

"Are you happy?" he asked. Claire had been adamant she wanted to do it. Patrick had taken convincing before he believed she wanted it enough to face it all alone.

"I am," she said and kissed his hand. "I really am. We're going to have a baby, Patrick."

The next day, when Claire came into his room, Patrick didn't answer her. For several minutes, Claire sat at the edge of his bed, occasionally whispering his name to be sure. But she knew he couldn't hear her anymore.

Claire never goes to her patients' funerals. She hadn't gone to Mr. Lui's funeral. And she did not go to Patrick's. Instead, she called in sick the day after he died. She ate two tubs of strawberry Häagen-Dazs ice cream, cried the entire day, and, in the evening, watched *Butch Cassidy and the Sundance Kid*, which Patrick had told her was his favourite movie, but which Claire had never seen.

By nightfall, it is raining again. The light from the streetlamps shines through the wet streaks and speckles on the windows, making a hundred small shadows dance against the room's pale walls.

"Who have you lost? Yourself, I mean," asks Mrs. Beasley. Twice a month, Claire works a weekend of night shifts. Mrs. Beasley knows she will be going tonight. She has, in her way, said all of her goodbyes already, and she has asked if Claire will sit with her. Claire has agreed to stay for as long as she can.

"Oh, I've lost a lot," says Claire. "Everyone does, I guess. It's part of life. People don't want to go around thinking of it like that—of death as travelling with us each step of the way, but it does. We begin. We live. We end. In between, if a person is lucky like you've been, they get to love a lot and to be loved. But, if you love a lot of people, some of them are bound to go before you, I guess."

"Such as for you?"

"Well, my mother, when I was little. Then, way later, my stepmother. And my grandparents, of course. Two of them before I was born, so that doesn't count as a loss, I guess, since I never knew them."

Claire sighs, shifts in the white plastic chair by Mrs. Beasley's bed. She is tired. Evening shifts are getting harder for her.

"Plus, my best friend growing up," she continues. She thinks of Thalma, her long, dark braids, always perfectly woven by Thalma's mother. She pictures herself and Thalma playing in their old school playground, hiding in the tire wells planted for climbing, telling stories and gossiping about boys. "And many other friends," she finishes. "A lot of friends like you."

Mrs. Beasley seems to consider Claire's list in the gentle, rain-pattered quiet of the room. Claire can hear one of the nurses walking quickly past the door and down the hall. A patient must have pressed a call button.

"I have been thinking about it, Claire, and you need to tell his family soon," the tiny woman says. "They have to have the choice."

"I know," answers Claire. "I've been putting it off. But I'm running out of time, I guess."

"We all do." Mrs. Beasley smiles. "But you are heading toward a start. A beautiful, little boy."

Mrs. Beasley's eyes are closed, but, in her smile, Claire can see the prettiness that once belonged to what must have been a very charming young woman. Mrs. Beasley's silky, white hair still holds natural curls that must, at one time, have been the envy of every girl in her school, and that must have looked lovely beneath a bridal veil, have been stroked and played with adoringly by her husband and her lover.

"I'm going to miss you, Mrs. B.," says Claire. The baby kicks just as a silent tear slides down Claire's cheek. She takes Mrs. Beasley's hand in her own, squeezes it gently. Mrs. Beasley squeezes back.

"Would you show me your memories?" asks Claire. "Just picture them."

And the old lady does. Parents, cousins, friends. Her first kiss, her second. Dances, barbeques, weddings—others', her own. Arguments. Funerals. Intimacy. Pleasure. Days at the beach with children. Fear and regret. The handing down of recipes. The hosting of parties. The holding of a hand as old and weathered as hers. A promise that they would see each other again. All the points where love and belonging have tied her world together.

The baby stirs again, a foot wedging against one of Claire's ribs.

Claire presses the morphine button to make Mrs. Beasley's last hour as painless as possible, pulls her blanket up to her shoulders to keep her warm. She whispers goodbye lightly enough to not disturb the old woman, who is immersed in her memories. Claire cannot afford to be in the room when Mrs. Beasley goes. She has already been on duty for too many deaths lately.

In the hallway, the soft, orange light from the sconces glows warmly, softening the medicinal sternness of the antiseptic green walls. Claire takes a deep breath, wishes Mrs. Beasley well, then finishes the rest of her rounds.

After Mrs. Beasley's funeral, Claire goes home to her apartment and stares at her phone for a full ten minutes before picking it up to phone Lisa, Patrick's sister. Patrick had given Claire the number. For seven months Claire has worried and worried at the idea until it became too overwhelming to consider actually doing, no matter how much she knew she needed to. But, she promised Patrick she would let his family know. And, she promised Mrs. Beasley she would do it soon.

"Here we go, little man," she says to her belly as she dials.

Patrick talked a lot about Lisa. Claire had even seen her, in passing, as she came in with her and Patrick's mother to visit every week or so. They couldn't watch him die. But, they couldn't stay away, either.

Lisa lives in a suburb in the south end, with her husband and an overenthusiastic black and white border collie that Patrick adored. Patrick had described Lisa's house to Claire, too. It was where the whole family would gather on special occasions, after their mother retired and moved out to one of the villages up the coast. Their father died of a heart attack when Lisa and Patrick were teenagers. Patrick said Lisa and he grew very close after that.

After the fifth ring, Lisa picks up. At first, she is confused about why Patrick's nurse would be calling so many months after his death. Then there is hesitation, the quietness of disbelief, followed by shock as Claire delivers the news.

"I knew him a long time ago, before the accident" says Claire, closing her eyes in dread. Her lie is ridiculous, but even with so much time to find a better one, she hasn't been able to. "He also came to a couple of times at the hospice, and we got to talking. No one wanted to get your hopes up, so we didn't tell you, but he told me he wanted this and we agreed on it. He told me a bunch of things about you, so you would know I was telling the truth if you needed any evidence. And I'm happy to do a DNA test if you like. I don't want anything. Just to—"

"You're really pregnant?" Lisa cuts off Claire's rambling spiral.

"Yes."

"And it is really, truly Patrick's?"

"I one hundred per cent promise. I loved him. And I believe he loved me. I'm sorry I didn't tell you before. I don't want anything. I just thought you had a right to know."

"What was his favourite colour?"

"Umber. He liked the word."

Claire hears Lisa start to cry, first in sniffles, and then in deep sobs that resonate wetly over the phone.

"Oh, my god," she says through gulps for breath, before her voice, at last, levels out again. "That is amazing, amazing news," she says. "When can I see you? What can we do?"

Claire sighs out the breath she had been holding. Lisa insists that, yes, both she and her mother will definitely want to be involved. It is the absolute best response Claire could have expected. She had braced herself for anger, for being turned away as a lunatic, or being accused of raping Patrick. The wave of gratitude she feels sends her sinking slowly to the floor, phone still in her hand, her other hand lightly rubbing her belly, sending happiness to the baby inside.

The two women talk for a long time about the baby and about Patrick, about what he would have wanted for the baby, about what Claire hopes for the baby, too.

"I'll put you as my contact for the hospital," Claire promises. "That way you can come see him as soon as he's born."

"Anything you need, you let us know," Lisa says.

"No, I'm good. In fact, my apartment is full of everything anyone would ever need to take care of a new baby."

"When are you due?"

"December third."

"Okay. I'll give my work the heads-up that I might have to leave suddenly sometime around then."

"You can tell them December third. Don't ask me how, but I'm absolutely certain it will be early in the morning, December third. And you should know that I want him to be named Patrick," says Claire. Her tears are slipping silently past her broad smile. They drip onto the fabric of her colourful tunic, making her stomach wet. "And, if anything happens, you know, during delivery..."

"Nothing's going to happen, Claire. You're young. You have nothing to worry about."

"I know. Thanks. But there's not really anyone else I can tell this to, so, just in case, I want you to know I've bought everything for him, and the key to my apartment and my address and everything will be in my suitcase for the hospital. It has little yellow flowers on it, if you can't find it."

"Claire, it's going to be fine."

"Yeah, I know. I'm just worried, I guess. But... I think he's going to be a great kid, Lisa. I'm really glad about how excited you are. I just know you're going to love him."

Anita Dolman

Refraction

Wave like an echo. Girl on the shore. Maybe twelve years old. Maybe older. Emerging from the water. The last of the day's light twirling pink ribbons among the ocean waters behind her.

I blink to disperse the ribbons, the girl, the illusion in the dimming light. The girl on the shore is still there, looking around to the north, then downshore, to the south. She is wet in jeans and T-shirt, but has no shoes on.

She is not the first illusion. I see things that are true, but there are times I see things that are not. I know that. I try not to see the things that aren't there, but sometimes they come all the same. I do not take the medicine stored in my bathroom cupboard, and so I keep seeing them. It is my choice, and I have my reasons. What I see harms no one. And my paintings support me.

I live mostly away from people, but that is also my choice. Lizzie comes to see me. She's real; she's my sister. She comes Fridays for dinner and other times to make arrangements or to take stock for potential clients or a gallery. But right now there is a girl on the shore.

The girl hugs herself. It's getting cooler, and the water could not have been warm to begin with. If she is real, she must be getting quite cold.

If she's real, where did she come from? Mine is the only house for nearly a kilometre in either direction. And the nearest island must be at least three kilometres out. I don't see a boat anywhere. She looks like she must be shivering.

"Girl!"

I've startled her. I walk down the sandy path between the shrubs and the small, sharp rocks slick with lichen so she can see me, so I will not be just a strange man's voice coming from the bushes.

"Girl, are you okay?"

She is staring at me. Perhaps she's not real after all. Normally, the fictions I see don't make sounds, and the ones I hear I can't see.

"I... I... Is this the mainland?"

"It is. How did you get here?"

"I swam. From our island. I had to... Where am I, exactly?"

"The nearest town is Gibsons, but it's some ways away. I live in the house over there. You swam from an island? To here?" I look out again from one tip of the shallow bay to the other and out beyond the ends of the peninsulas that frame my world. I don't see a raft or anything at sea on which she could have sailed or floated or paddled. She is soaked through, her long hair dripping large, slowing drops of saltwater into the sand at her feet. I'm close enough now to see that she truly is shivering.

"Come to the house. You can warm up," I say.

She stares at me again from where she stands, as if she is also trying to figure out if I am real, or—if real—a threat.

"I'm not a danger," I tell her, although saying so cannot, of course, make this seem less of a possibility to her. "Crazy, maybe." I begin to smile, then stop myself in fear that this would look lecherous or forboding in the lonely evening light. "But not dangerous."

"Okay," she says.

At the house, I leave her dripping ocean water onto my mat while I gather a stack of bath towels from the linen closet. While she dries off in the bathroom, I put on water for hot chocolate and make her a cheese sandwich, ringing the plate with pepper-and-lime potato chips. I give her an old shirt and sweater of mine and find a pair of Lizzie's socks and yoga pants, all far too big for her.

Once she is dressed, I bring the girl a blanket to curl up in on the couch while I run her clothes through the dryer. She is very quiet. I'm not sure what to do next, or what I should be asking her. What is a person supposed to do when a girl washes ashore on their beach like flotsam? She accepts the CBC mug and the sandwich plate, and says "Thank you" with a courteous nod. She blows at the brown bubbles like birthday candles and begins to drink the steaming chocolate in tiny sips.

I start a fire in the fireplace. I don't usually. I rarely trust myself to remember I have started a fire, unless I am having a very good day. Today was not a bad day, but I keep a steady watch on the girl all the same, just to make sure she's still there. I notice she's eaten the entire sandwich and has set the plate back down on the coffee table, although she has so far left the chips mostly untouched.

"What did you mean you're crazy, maybe?" she asks after another small slurp from her drink.

"What did you mean you swam here?" I ask.

"I asked you first."

"I'm schizophrenic. I don't take my medication so I can keep making paintings like those over there. I've never hurt anyone, and I don't imagine I ever would. I just sometimes see and hear things that aren't really there. I can normally tell which they are, though, so I get by alright."

"Did you, like, actually paint those?"

"I did."

"They're amazing. And big. Do people buy them and stuff?"

"They do. I have a website, and my sister's my agent. People seem to want them. There are times I'm not sure why. Sometimes I get the sense they don't see in them exactly what I do. Other times I feel they must, or something close to it. Your turn. Why are you here?"

The girl draws her legs in beneath the blanket and lets out a sigh. It catches in the middle.

"You're going to think I'm totally nuts," she says. She looks toward the floor-to-ceiling windows framing the now lightless shoreline.

She tells me a story too big to believe, too complicated not to. Her name, she says, is Rebecca. She has rarely left her family's private island before, but for a few trips to a mainland doctor or with her father on grocery runs when she was smaller, or, more recently, to come in for homeschool testing.

She tells me she grew up on her family's one-house island with her parents and four older siblings—two sisters and two brothers, none of them allowed to go off the island without the permission of their father, and, even then, the girls only allowed to go under his direct supervision. Her father commutes to a job on the mainland. Her two brothers have done odd jobs and mechanical work in towns along the coast.

"Father always treated Mom like some kind of maid or something," she tells me. "She'd have to scrub all the floors, start cooking as soon as the sun came up, feed the chickens, even teach us spelling and math. Plus what Father calls 'proper living.' You know, the right rules for everything from how to stay clean, to how women have to be devoted to their men and make them happy—starting with their fathers, and then, later on, the husband he picks for her.

Rebacca's face has grown flush as she has become more emphatic. She leans forward.

"It was totally insane," she says. "We knew other people didn't live like this. We would sneak in and watch Father's TV in his den, or listen to my brother's radio. Sometimes, if no one else was around, Mom would tell the girls about the world outside and about her life before she married Father."

Rebecca goes on. When she was five, she says, her eldest brother turned eighteen. For his birthday, their father brought him home a wife. The pretty ,young woman had been part of a religious group from the interior mainland, and Rebecca thinks their father had bought her from her own family. A pastor from the girl's sect came to the island to officiate the wedding. Rebecca's father built the new couple an extension on the main house.

Rebecca's brother soon announced his new bride was pregnant. Within days, though, says Rebecca, her father made another announcement at dinner as well. Rebecca's eldest sister, Ruby, was pregnant, too. She was sixteen. Their father was proud and beaming, with Ruby ensconced in her new seat next to him. That same week, he turned the windowless attic into a bedroom. He moved his wife into it, and his daughter into his own bedroom.

"She just had her fourth," Rebecca tells me. "It's gross; I know." Her mug is empty, and I offer her a glass of water from the kitchen. I bring it to her. She watches me carefully, says a quiet "Thanks" before returning to her story.

"Roxanne, my other sister, turned fifteen last year and Father bought this huge, king-sized bed and moved it into his bedroom so she could move in there with him and Ruby. She didn't want to, though, so he tied her up in the dining room and kept her there for almost three weeks—day and night—so we could all see how awful she was to go against what he said was 'nature's command.'"

What Rebecca's story lacks in persuasiveness it makes up for in peculiarity. The reality she paints is far removed from my small world and the various and ever-changing truths that fill my canvases. I've followed along closely, though, and my math comes up one sibling short, so I play along. "You said you had two brothers. What happened to the other?"

Rebecca sets her glass down on the coffee table. She is gazing into the water, or at the firelight reflecting on the glass. I remember to get up and add a log to the fire.

"He didn't want to live like the rest of us. Like Father. He tried to leave after Father took Ruby as his daughter-wife. I guess he had built a kind of little powerboat. I don't know why he didn't just run off and stay on the mainland one of the times Father took him to work at the mechanic's. Maybe he wanted his stuff. Anyway, Father caught him that night as he was pushing out. He wouldn't even let us have, like, a funeral for him. He just sank the body out in the ocean with something heavy."

Rebecca lets out another sigh, another hitch, looking down all the while.

I notice the firelight reflected in the windows and consider the sea beyond.

"Won't your father be looking for you?"

"No."

Her answer is immediate and far more severe than I would have thought a preteen should be able to manage.

When I was a boy, I was normal. I had friends. I did things. I never saw the things that aren't there. Lizzie is a couple of years younger than me, and we didn't often enjoy the same things, but she and I both loved renting old Hitchock movies, black and white thrillers, film noir. Ashen ladies in veiled hats, men in fedoras uncovering clues down by the pier. Secret jewels and long-lost heirs and hidden bullets.

"Girl," I ask. "What happened today?"

"Well, I don't know how the teachers found out about us, but last year they started getting Mom to use this province curriculum stuff to teach me, with these special books and everything. We had to come to the mainland for me to do these homeschool tests twice a year. Mid-terms and finals. Anyway, I started learning all this stuff about science, and geography, and history, and about biology and people. And, at the same time I also got talking to Ruby and Roxanne, and I realized Father makes us his wives when we each, you know, become, like, *fertile*. And I guess Mom knew this, because I guess she got booted out when she, well, wasn't anymore. So Mom took me to do the mid-terms last week. Father brought us, but they said Mom had to come because she was the teacher, and anyway, I guess she ended up having this moment alone with one of the school board people, and she must have told them something because yesterday these people from the Ministry of Children and Family Development came out to the house."

"No one was expecting it, not even Mom, I think. Father wasn't home, but my brother made us all act like everything was normal, like we were just one big, happy family. It looked like the lady and the guy bought the whole thing, but then it all got worse right away."

Rebecca has been speaking faster and faster, and now she takes a breath. She looks out the windows again, to the darkness masking the sea, but I keep watching the changes in her expression from sentence to sentence, the rise and fall of her eyebrows as she talks.

"When Father came home, my brother told him what had happened. Father figured out right away it was because of Mom."

For the first time, Rebecca loses the strange, unteenaged calm that has so far lent a surreal quality to her story. A crease etches itself onto her forehead, and her eyes start to glisten in the flickering, orange light. I can tell she wants desperately for me to believe what she is telling me.

"My brother held me back in the living room while Father taught us all what happens to wives who disrespect their husbands. He strangled her right in front of us. With his hands. No one else even moved or said anything, except for the little kids, who were all crying and screaming. My Mom looked right at me before he did it, and then I could tell she was trying to look away from everyone. I think it was probably so none of us would, you know, be the one to watch her go."

Rebecca is rocking slightly back and forth on the couch, her knees drawn up again before her. If I do believe her, I wonder what she expects I will, or can, do with the information that she is giving me?

"I couldn't let him do that," she says. "He took her out and sunk her like he did with Ryan. Like she was garbage."

"That was last night?" I ask.

"Yeah, last night. And today everyone is pretending like everything is all normal; like it's all fine that our father just murdered our mom. Everyone is treating him all day with all this respect. Like it's just a nice, sunny Saturday except that for some mysterious reason Mom's not around."

"And tonight?"

"This evening, at dinner, he announces Roxanne is pregnant with her second. Everyone is clapping and Roxanne's trying to look like she's happy about it, and Father says a bunch of things about new beginnings. After dinner, he commands me to come with him outside. I can tell Roxanne and Ruby have this anxious look as I get up to go with him."

For the first time in her telling, I feel real pity for Rebecca, although I'm not sure whether it's for what she has already told, or what she is about to.

"So, he takes me out to the boat," she continues. "He traded the old one in a while back for this yacht-like thing, with a whole apartment in it. I guess he figured his own bedroom would be getting crowded soon. Anyway, he starts the boat, and we head out into the strait. I'm not usually alone with him. Plus, with what he just did to Mom, I'm completely freaked out, but he tells me to sit, and I do."

"After a while, he stops the boat. I can still see the island, but it's just a spot between two other islands that no one lives on. He tells me he figured I'd want to know where my mother was buried, and he nods out to a spot past the railing. Then he tells me her greatest sin against nature wasn't that she brought in the outside world but that she hid when each of us were ready. He says she knew it was my duty to help provide him with as many children as nature sees fit to give him. So now I know he knows, and he's coming up to me. We're by the stairs to go below, and I can tell what he's planning on doing. He starts saying how it's time for me to become his daughter-wife, and then he even jokes that he's short a wife now because of me. Then his hands are on my shoulders to turn me around and guide me down the stairs. I can smell his breath, and I'm picturing Mom out there in the water, and how I don't want to become like Ruby, so I secretly pull out the steak knife I'd brought with me from dinner from the side of my jeans. I make like I'm turning in to hug him. For a second he looks like he's glad it's going to be so easy, and then it just goes right in."

"I thought it would be tougher, but it was easier than cutting up a chicken. But then he starts to flail around and swear and he grabs at me. He's down on his knees, so I start kicking and kicking, and I'm kicking him so much that first I kick him in chest, and then the eye, and then I'm kicking the knife in further and then there's all this blood coming from his mouth, too, and it's all bubbling and he's thrashing, and then he's not."

The fireplace crackles, and I get up to put on another log. I nudge the ashes around with the poker to build up more heat. My back still turned to her, I ask "So, you killed him."

"I killed him."

"If you had the boat," I ask, feeling like Humphrey Bogart, "why did you swim?"

A giggle comes from the direction of the couch.

"Mister, I'm thirteen. Even if I was old enough to drive a boat, it's not like Father would have taught me how." A look of insolent bitterness contorts her face. It is the first look she has given tonight that I recognize as belonging on a teenager.

"Since I couldn't drive the boat," she says, "I found some matches, and I tried to set it on fire. It didn't take at first, so I got his secret booze from the cabin, and I poured it all over the wood parts and tried again."

I put the poker back in its bin and close the fireplace grate. I look out toward the sea, at the reflection of the glowing firelight in the window. Have all of tonight's flames been reflected from inside?

"And you swam the whole way here?"

"I swim lots. I'm really good. It's all there was to do at home."

A buzzer rings.

"That's the dryer," I tell her. "It's in the bathroom if you want your clothes. You're welcome to stay the night, though. You could use what you're wearing as pyjamas if you like."

"Yes, please," she says once more, as deferential as at the start. I tell her where I keep spare toothbrushes in the medicine cabinet, and she heads to the bathroom to get ready for the night.

I unfold the couch to make her a bed. I think about *The Maltese Falcon*, about dark grey mysteries within mysteries. Lizzie and I used to always guess at who the killer was, where the treasure would be hidden, what the underlying mystery might be. Sometimes, Lizzie was right. But I never was. I think now that I enjoyed them because they were nothing like the way my mind has ever worked. They offered clear resolutions, however concealed the path leading to them may have been. Back then, I didn't see what wasn't there. But I seemed to be able to think of every conceivable ending without guessing at which the writer would have preferred. With everything a possible clue, how can anyone know which detail will lead to revelation?

I spread sheets from the linen closet across the bed, tuck them in at the edges. Returning to my room for a pillow, I notice the bathroom door is ajar.

"Girl?" I call. There's no answer, and I push the door wider. The dryer is empty, the bathroom window slightly open, as it had been before Rebecca arrived.

I go back to the great room. A fire is still burning in the fireplace. A half-drained glass of water sits on the coffee table. I can see a CBC mug and a plate of chips on the kitchen counter.

From the laneway, I hear the tires of a car slowly grinding their way up the gravel drive, and my heart skips and then settles. Less than a minute later, there is a knock on the door.

The policeman would like to know if I have seen a runaway. About thirteen years old. Named Beth. Her parents are very worried. She took a boat from their island.

"Sorry," I say. "I don't see much of anyone out here. I hope she's okay. Her parents must be frantic."

"They are. She's the oldest of a whole brood, and it sounds like they're all pretty worried. Seems she's a bit of a troublemaker, but still, you know? Anyway, give us a call if you see anything."

I spot the bowl on the ledge where I normally keep my things for the outside world. My watch. My loose money. My pocket knife. My compass. All gone, except for my house keys.

"Will do, officer. Good luck," I say. I close the door and wait for the sound of a car heading toward the road.

I turn off the lights and go to the bank of windows to watch the girl on the shore walking along the water, wave like an echo, the indigo ray of the moon on the sea behind her a good colour for tomorrow.

Anita Dolman

Bed and Breakfast

Lift the dough from the bowl, pound and pound, then roll. More flour, pound and roll again.

The guests will be here soon. And Wally, too. Wally is also a guest, but he has stayed so often it feels as though he belongs. He pays his bill each time, though. In cash, with a tip. Twenty per cent. It's way too much, and Helen has told him so, but that's Wally.

He can't be making much money as a travelling salesman, even if he travels around selling fancy electronic gadgets to big companies. Helen has asked him about the gadgetry before, but she's not one for computers, and she stopped hearing him after he began to talk about harnessing fluctuations.

She should ask him, though, how his company does. Not that it's her business. He is a guest, and a question like that would be crossing a line. Helen tries not to pry with guests. Although that's not always easy. So many are young couples in love, and she senses their lives must be filled with romance and adventure.

Romance and adventure. That's what Helen's B&B is supposed to offer. It says so on the website Wally made for her. Really, it's up to the guests to arrange their own romance or adventure. Helen just offers the setting. The big farmhouse, its baseboards painted white, softwood floors, the flowered wallpaper different in each room.

A little balcony stretches out from the back of each of the two suites, offering a full view of the final row of foothills, the soaring mountains beyond. Their slopes and fissures fill with shadows and light, the mottled rock glowing copper in

71

the morning, then cast in dark crimson against the pink party dress of the evening sky.

Three horses, the colour of mahogany, roam the wildflowers and grass below. They belong to Arnold, who has leased Helen's pasture for the past few years. Helen's golden retriever, Omega, yaps in protest at some real or imagined prairie dog beyond the garden.

The B&B is only open on weekends. While they're here, Helen's guests get full access to the land and all the countless paths worn by decades of city couples hoping to see whatever they have come to see. Passersby can't see the house from the highway, just the sign by the road. Then it's a long turn around the hill before they arrive at the gravel parking bed next to the house. Wally usually arrives first. He has come nearly every weekend for two years.

Helen can hear the first car pulling up. The guests always drive up in little city cars, so Helen can tell it's Wally by the heavy, slow movement of his relic of a car as it pulls into the furthest spot. Wally likes to leave the closer spots for what he calls "the real guests."

Helen lifts the bowl of dough to the windowsill to let it rise again. She checks her earrings to make sure they're straight and haven't escaped into the mixing bowl. She cleans the counters as she hears the screen door open, the wheels of Wally's suitcase bumping over the threshold.

"Hi honey, I'm home," he calls.

"Hello dear," she calls in response. "How was work?"

"Oh, same old, same old." Wally is at the archway to the kitchen, but Helen keeps her back to him. She wants the game to last as long as possible before the mood inevitably breaks, and Wally goes to his room to unpack.

"I brought you something," he says.

"Oh, Wally, you shouldn't have."

Helen turns. Wally usually brings her supplies for the B&B, or something for herself that she has asked for from the city— material for new curtains or a watch battery or a book. In his right hand, he is holding the berry sugar for which she asked. In his other hand, he is holding a wrapped package. The paper is a pale pink, with stripes of shimmering, metallic white.

Helen wipes her hands on her apron and takes the package. She hears a second car come up the drive.

"Open it later," Wally says. His smile is sly. Something is definitely up, but Helen thanks him for the sugar and puts both items in a cupboard.

This weekend's couple is Norwegian, Aesa and Norman Brege-something. They are getting married in the fall, they say. The weekend is a break from preparations, or at least from Aesa's mother, who, as Norman tells Wally, "has taken the helm but seems to be steering for the rocks."

Helen thinks it's peculiar they would come all the way to the Canadian Rockies for only a few days, rather than save a trip like this for a honeymoon, but, as ever, she feels she shouldn't pry.

Helen has had visitors from what feels like every country. She has started to wonder how so many people can have so much extra money to afford random weekend getaways to the middle of nowhere, when she herself has known very few people rich enough to do such a thing. But then, she thinks, maybe it's just that she has known so few people, or that those she's known have mostly lived in her small patch of the world, with its struggles of land and changing weather and the perpetual loss of grown children to the lure of the cities.

She imagines her little website reaching around the globe with its promise of fresh bread, a hillside garden full of strawberries and pink bleeding hearts, and the calming guarantee of no more than two sets of guests at any time.

Nearly every one of her guests has been quiet and polite, all of them interested in her life "out here:" the types of plants, her baking, the house itself, the scenery. Of course, there have been some odd guests, such as the young, single man who watched TV in the living room the entire weekend, planting himself on the worn, green sofa the moment he walked in behind Wally. Helen can't recall if he ever made it to his bedroom or looked out a window at any point. But he, too, said his thank yous, paid his bill, and told Helen her biscuits, which he ate on the couch, dusting the crumbs into a napkin while never taking his eyes from the television, were "brilliant."

Norman has thinning, vellum-blond hair. His wife-to-be is not short, but Norman has to duck to pass through their bedroom doorway.

At dinner, they ask the usual questions, and Helen provides the usual answers between receiving compliments on the lamb, the lemon asparagus, the balsamic Parisian potatoes. Over the years, Helen's friends and, most enthusiastically, her husband, John, often told her she was a marvellous cook. After John died five years ago, Helen was alright financially, between the insurance and the settlement from the oil company, but, after a while, she started to think a business, especially one where she could cook for others again, would help ease her loneliness. Arnold was the one who suggested a B&B.

"Since 1988," she answers Norman. "My husband and I bought this as a sort of a hobby farm, but he died in an industrial accident. He was a foreman on an oil crew."

Does Helen have children? Does she spend all her time on the farm, or does she get to town sometimes? What is the town like? Is it an older population, or are there young families? Does Helen have a lot of friends? What do people in the town do for entertainment? Does she grow these potatoes herself? How?

During these conversations, Helen feels like a tour guide to her own life. She marvels again at how her life can be interesting enough for guests to want to know so much about it. Even with the barrage of questions, she often senses there are other things the guests would like to ask, but don't. She can't imagine what they wouldn't ask, since they already ask so many things. Perhaps they want to know about her income? About living alone? Certainly no one would ask her anything to do with sex. But what else is still taboo?

No, she has no children. Yes, she has lived away from here—the year in Calgary before she met John. She gets to town every month or so. Her neighbour, Arnold, brings her groceries once a week. And Wally brings her anything else she wants from the city. Twice a year or so she goes to the nearest city, Lethbridge. Once, she went to New York, on her honeymoon.

She omits the plans she once had to travel far, to see all the places that now send her their young couples in love. In the time before John bought the land. Before the ticking of the clock stitched them both into place. Before she became old without noticing, and even the idea that she had once wanted to see the world became more difficult for her to believe.

Then the inevitable questions about New York, when she went, what it was like. Helen has bought several guide books and histories of New York so she can answer more knowledgably. Now, she's no longer sure how much of the attractions, the restaurants, the people are from what she remembers from her one week and how much are from books.

"Of course, I don't have to go anywhere nowadays," she jokes. "The whole world seems determined to come to me."

Wally laughs kindly, as he does every Friday when she says it.

After dinner, Wally helps with the dishes.

"You know you don't have to," Helen tells him once more.

"And you know I will anyway," Wally answers. "Say, where did you put my package?"

"Oh, heavens," Helen rinses the last dinner plate and dries her hands quickly, "I can't believe I forgot."

"You must not get enough presents, then," says Wally, drying the plate and stacking it in the cupboard.

Helen pulls the package down from its hiding place. Now that she has a moment for investigation, she can tell the gift has the weight and shape of a hardcover book.

"No!" Helen says with a breath of excitement. "You got it!" Charlotte Davis's next Departures and Arrivals book. Claire-Anne is Helen's favourite protagonist, the pilot of a small plane, travelling around the world in search of great adventure and spiritual calm.

The metallic wrapping already in shreds on the counter, Helen pulls at the yellow tissue paper beneath.

"I've heard it's the best yet," says Helen. "The last one was a bit slower than the others, but the review in the *Herald* said she's really back with this one."

The title is embossed in silver letters across the image of an airport lounge, planes taking off and landing on a night runway visible through plate glass windows reflecting the comings and goings of passengers and crews. *Flight of Whimsy.* It's not the title she expected.

"Is it alright?" Wally asks.

"Sorry? Oh, yes. Yes, absolutely. It's wonderful. I can't wait to read it. Thank you, Wally."

Helen stretches herself up on her toes and gives Wally a peck on the cheek. As she pulls back, she sees he is turning red.

"Well, I knew you liked them, and I saw it in the store, so I just thought..."

"You thought very kindly, Wally."

From the corner of her nightstand, the book tugs at Helen's attention as she gets ready for bed. Her room has the only en-suite bathroom in the house. She could likely charge more for it than for either of the other rooms, but it allows her privacy with which she is not willing to part.

Helen crawls into bed and lays the book on her lap. She runs her fingers over the smooth, molded letters. Embossing makes her think of people's instinct to etch their presence: Cavemen carving in stone before there were alphabets, before, perhaps, there were even many words. Teenagers scratching their names and romances into trees and picnic tables. The graduating class of 1987 carving a giant "87" into the rocks beside the railway bridge a few kilometres down the highway. How do they tell their children to behave, when a lasting emblem of their own insolence is engraved above the highway where they drive them to school each day?

Helen turns the book over. She reads the synopsis. She turns it to the front, opens the cover, reads the first paragraph. There is no question now. This is not the next book in the series. Helen owns all seven books published so far. The newest came out two days ago. *Flight of Beauty.* Claire-Anne is still with Charlie at the start, because that is where the last one ended. The *Herald* reviewer even mentioned they are still together in the first chapter.

But, in *Flight of Whimsy*, of which Helen has never heard, Claire-Anne is with someone named Rudolpho. She has left the Malaysian Cargo Co. to start a business giving aerial tours of the Brazilian rainforest. The blurb on the back reads "Book #9 in Davis's Departures and Arrivals series."

Maybe Wally got hold of an advance copy of the following book. But how could they have an advance copy this far ahead of time? Maybe they released them simultaneously. Helen turns to the copyright page.

Helen puts the book on the nightstand. She stares at it for a long time before turning off the light. She will ask Wally in the morning where he got the book.

The guests are up early. Helen can hear them moving around upstairs, but the weather is good, so they will likely spend time on the balcony before coming down for breakfast.

Helen puts the dough in the oven. Wally is already outside fiddling with her barbecue, which he promised last weekend he would try to fix, against Helen's protests. Wally says he has trouble sleeping, so he's usually up around the same time as Helen. She meant to ask Arnold to look at the barbecue, but he was in a hurry this week when he dropped off the groceries. He was off to see about another horse, this one abandoned by owners who had skipped out on their rent in the night. The callousness of people who abandon animals they had promised to care for bothers Helen more than nearly any other human failing. Arnold's compassion for abused horses made him one of Helen's favourite people from the time they met. When he came by after John died and told her he had bought the old Bowler ranch down the road, she was happy to rent him extra corral space for his rescued horses.

Helen starts cracking the eggs for her specialty "garden-fresh omelette."

"Sorry, Helen."

Startled, Helen drops half an eggshell into the mixture.

"Wally," she gasps in exasperation. "You scared the life out of me."

She picks most of the shell out, but several shards have drifted to the bottom of the bowl.

"Sorry. I was trying not to slam the door, in case the guests are still sleeping. I was just coming in to apologize for not being a barbecue salesman. I've looked at it every which way, and all I can tell you is that I think something is loose, but I can't see what."

Helen fishes the last eggshell fragments out with a decorative teaspoon.

"That's okay. Thank you for trying. I'll ask Arnold to take a look this week. I'll just roast the fish in the oven tonight. And don't worry about the guests—I already heard them stirring."

Helen slides diced peppers, tomatoes, and zucchini from the cutting board into the bowl. Wally is washing his hands.

"Wally," Helen starts from behind the fridge door, "that book you got me... could there have been some kind of printing error?"

"What do you mean? Are there pages missing?" Wally is drying his hands on Helen's tea towel, which she has explained to him several times is only for dishes.

"No, nothing like that. It's just..." Helen looks at Wally for a long time. Wally is the same Wally as ever. "I think I must be missing the book in between—the one before this one, I mean."

For a fragment of an instant, she thinks she sees his eyes widen. There is a tiny sound and Helen wonders if Wally has hiccupped.

"I must have gotten it wrong," says Helen, "the name of the one that just came out. Never mind, though. This one looks great. I don't mind skipping ahead."

"I'm sorry," says Wally.

To Helen, the staring contest has become uncomfortable, and she wishes one of them would look away, but she can't seem to break Wally's gaze. He starts to dry his hands again.

"I don't know how that happened," he says. "It must have been a printing error, like you said."

Aesa and Norman are coming down the stairs.

"It's okay," says Helen, turning the coffee maker on. "It really isn't a problem. I appreciate it either way."

After breakfast, Aesa and Norman head out to the trails with a copy of the homemade map Wally made with Helen's help after one of the couples got lost last year. Wally and Helen went with Omega to find them after they didn't return for dinner, but they had to turn back at dusk to avoid getting lost themselves. In the end, Arnold went out on one of the horses and brought the couple back in the dark.

"I'm going to see if I can spot any osprey today," says Wally. It's the first thing he has said to her since they talked about the book. He has his jacket on and is putting one of Helen's chocolate granola bars into his birding kit. "I probably won't be back before four. I'll see you later."

Helen has prepared all the dinner side dishes in advance, so with Wally gone, she has a rare Saturday break. Wally takes care of her website using his own computer, checking with Helen and answering any potential guests' questions on her behalf. Now Helen wishes she had a computer of her own. She could find answers quickly when she has questions. She decides she will buy one and get Wally to set it up. Perhaps she will take one of the introductory courses at the community centre in town. It's been a long time since she has taken a class.

Helen finds the book review in the recycle bin. *Flight of Beauty*. Book #8. She knew, but needed to see it written again. She takes the entire reviews section of the paper and slides it into her nightstand drawer. She looks out the bedroom window to the hills to see if she can see either Wally or the couple. Even Omega isn't in view, or earshot.

She hears a knock on the front door. Helen can see Arnold through the screen before she is all the way down the stairs. She knows he must have taken in the horse.

"Do you have him already?" she asks, opening the door.

"I'm going to bring him Tuesday, if it's alright with you."

"Of course, it's alright," says Helen. "Come on in."

Arnold holds the door open with the back of his hand, but doesn't come in.

"I can't stay long, I'm afraid, Helen. I was coming to give you a head's-up about the new gelding, and actually to see Wally, too. Is he in?"

"He's birding."

"Birding?"

"I know. He doesn't seem the type, does he? He goes a fair bit, though. He said he's after osprey today, won't be back until about four. I think he usually heads south. I imagine he goes along the creek. He's—" Helen stops herself.

"What?" he asks.

"Oh... nothing, really." Helen feels flustered. She tries never to talk too much about Arnold to Wally, or about Wally to Arnold, although they are friendly with each other, if not completely friends. She doesn't want either one of them to get the impression anything untoward is happening between her and the other. "He just doesn't seem quite himself today," she says.

Arnold gives a generic, cowboy-esque grunt.

"Well, if you see him, tell him to come my way."

"Of course."

Arnold has ridden out of sight on his own horse, Mange, before Helen realizes she has forgotten again to ask him about the barbecue.

Helen picks up a copy of the homemade map. The solid white lines mark the laneway, the highway to the east, and a series of connected, mostly abandoned oil company roads to the west. A long row of tiny waves bobbing back and forth along the map marks the creek and its tributaries, which, beyond the map, ultimately lead to the river. Wally drew peaks for the mountains that can be seen to the west, with a name written at the base of each upside-down V. Dotted lines show cattle trails or map out the walks Helen used to take with John. Helen studies Wally's sketch of the house, the garden, and the corral at the centre of the map. For five years, she has not put a foot outside of this section of the map, except for the rare errands to town or the city.

In the back of the hall closet, Helen finds her hiking shoes, tucked next to John's steel-toed boots. The hikers feel new, even though they were well broken in by the time John passed. Helen hasn't worn them since the company men came to tell her about the explosion.

At the top of the nearest hill, she finds Omega, trying her best to roust a warren of hares.

"Let's go for a walk, old girl," says Helen. She snaps her fingers. Within seconds, Omega has circled her twice and is four feet ahead as they aim for one of their old favourite paths, down to the creek and along the little valley winding between the closest foothills.

Two kilometres from the house, and the air smells vibrant with wildflowers and fresh, flowing water. Indian paintbrush has coloured the fields red and orange on the far side of the creek. Congregations of white yarrow sway in the breeze, knocking gently against Helen's legs as she walks.

Helen thought she would start to miss John fiercely the moment she stepped onto the trail. Instead, she feels steadily calmer as she goes. Listening to the breeze rustle the tall grasses, she feels an incredible connection, not just to John, but to everything around her she has shut out since he died.

Stopping to watch the creek's eddies swirl through the rocky bend in front of the next hill, Helen hears a churning sound and then a zap. Omega doesn't look up from lapping water at the shore. Helen hears the noise again.

"Omega, what is that?" Omega looks up, but doesn't come to Helen.

"Omega, girl, come along."

The dog saunters up the slope as Helen follows the sound.

When Helen rounds the hill, she cannot, at first, make sense of what she sees. She wonders if the oil company has come onto her land without permission to dig a giant hole. She discards the idea as quickly as it appeared. She's never heard of an oil company doing such a thing. Moreover, it's not a well, but a sort of cave carved into the side of the foothill.

Omega bounds for the opening. Helen shouts after her, but Omega disappears into the dark gash. An electrical hum is radiating from the entrance. Helen watches and listens, then carefully follows.

Just past the darkened mouth of the cave is a machine, roughly eight feet high. It looks strangely like an elevator, except that it is not attached to any shaft. Instead, it is sitting atop a large, metal dais. The room has clearly been carved into the hill, but the floor is a smooth, shiny, metallic white. It reminds Helen of the wrapping paper from Wally's book. The equally smooth walls are, bizarrely, decorated with a mural of what looks like a ranch scene at sunset.

By the time Wally arrives, Helen is seated on the office chair in front of the large panel of monitors and control boards. She is reading what looked to her at first like a rule book for some sort of role-playing game. Next to the controls is a small office table with an open tub of dog treats, presumably for Omega, who knew just where to find them. Also on the desk is a pile of brochures and several copies of the rule book, its cover a scene of wildflowers against a summery mountain backdrop.

"Where do they come from?" asks Helen. Wally looks terrible. His shirt is torn near the collar, above the open zipper of his jacket. His grey hair is messy, and there is a dark purple semicircle under his left eye. He doesn't answer.

"Where, Wally? Where do they come from?" The calm Helen had found walking the fields has turned strange and foreboding to her. Wally opens his mouth to speak, stops, then starts again.

"They come from all over. Just like they tell you. New England, Toronto, Amsterdam, Spain. Norway."

"Fine." Helen feels Wally is playing with her. "Then what do they come from, Wally? Or when? Or are you an insane old man who just built a particularly fancy closet in my hill to store birding gear?"

The corners of Wally's mouth sneak up for a moment, but his eyes look wet and worried.

"This is what I was trying to avoid," he says. "The answer to your question is *when*. And they're from the same *when* that I'm from," he says. "A long time from now, when things aren't as... clean, as good as they are here, for you."

"As good as they are for me..." Helen considers the past five years in one breath. What she has read in the guide book is ridiculous. What is in her hill is ridiculous. Wally is ridiculous.

"Then why me, Wally? Why am I a tourist attraction for your future? Does a bomb eventually land in my corral? Or am I just the perfect woman of the past? Come watch the humble widow tend her garden."

"You are... were... isolated. And friendly. And in a beautiful location. And you were open to it. Arnold just had to come here to convince you. And then I just had to set it up and keep it going."

"Arnold is in on this?"

"He's my boss. I live at his ranch most weeks. The travel takes its toll, so I don't usually go back that often. Arnold actually isn't supposed to be on this side as much as he is. The idea was just that he would set it up and then come check in occasionally."

Helen considers the bruise on Wally's face.

"Where is Arnold right now?" she asks.

"He's doing better than I am. He's getting Aesa and Norman. He wants to cut our losses and set up somewhere else. I thought I could still cover my mistake with you. It was such a tiny thing, really. But I imagine it's too late for that now." The look behind his sheepish grin is sad. For a moment, Helen wishes she had never discovered this ludicrous and impossible thing. It is more likely that Wally and Arnold really are insane. But, then, so much else would make sense if it were true. All of the guests. All of the questions.

"Look, I—" Wally moves toward Helen, then sees the shotgun by her side. If Wally had ever known Helen to take a walk in the fields, he would know that, when she walked alone, she always carried her gun, slung in a gun strap across her back. With Helen's back to the console, the gun was pointing to the floor, hidden along the shadowed folds of Helen's long skirt. "Helen."

"Wally." Helen leaves the gun pointing down, but keeps Wally's gaze. Their charming game feels long gone, and he like an imposter.

"Are there a lot of these 'destinations of the past,' Wally, or am I an exclusive attraction?"

"There are a couple now. Still very few. It's a start-up technology, and we've had some... legal issues."

"I would think so."

"Which we have been trying to overcome by minimizing our impact."

"Through the selection of widows living in the middle of nowhere."

"Through strict ethical standards," says Wally. He looks desperate for her to believe him, his eyes pleading, his hair still dishevelled from the fight. "But I broke the rules. I started getting personally involved in your life. Arnold felt I could possibly affect the trajectory of your life, which our rules say we absolutely cannot do. It's our golden rule of inter-era travelling."

There were times when Wally's mere arrival had made Helen feel light and excited. But, Helen wondered, if it wasn't for Wally, and for Arnold, and the guests, would she have stayed in the house as long as she had? Or would she have been more able to move on, to try to find out who she was without John, without the memories of their past together surrounding her? With the distraction of the B&B, it had taken her five years to go for a walk. Where could she have ended up instead if this idea hadn't kept her here, kept her "isolated," as Wally had said?

Norman is the first to come in, carrying his and his fiancée's suitcase. He is followed by Aesa, carrying their other bag. Arnold nearly walks into the young bride as she stops abruptly in the entrance, gaping at Helen. This sort of situation, Helen knows, having read it, does not come up in the *Traveller's Guide to Inter-Era Travel and Southern Alberta Customs of the Early 21st Century.*

"Don't worry," Helen says to Aesa. She nudges the butt of the gun outward like the top of a cane, so everyone can see it's there, but also that it's currently aimed to the ground. "All you need to do is go home. I wish you a very happy wedding. And all the best with your mother-in-law, Norman." Helen nods as a sign of well-meaning to the towering, frightened man.

"Please make them go now," she says to Wally.

"Helen—" Arnold starts.

"You know," says Helen, "I doubt I've heard my name this many times in a row in years. How lucky I am to draw so much attention from my two dearest friends."

The fake elevator door opens surprisingly much like an elevator door. Norman and Aesa, still cautious and gripping their luggage, walk inside. As the door closes, Norman casts Arnold a look that shows he and his bride-to-be are not happy with their vacation experience. Wally presses a series of buttons on the console.

A churning noise starts around the elevator, followed by a soft clicking, and then a zap. The elevator doors open again, revealing an empty chamber. Both remaining men turn to Helen at the same moment.

"I never meant to hurt you, Helen," says Arnold. His head is tilted to the side, his expression clenched. Helen sees that he believes he's being honest. "I can tell you both Wally's and my friendship with you were sincere."

"Wally says your golden rule is not to interfere with someone's life," says Helen.

"And he's right. Wally will be dealt with when we return to our time."

"What happens if you do interfere with the past?"

"Well, it can change the future, of course, although not nearly as dramatically as you might think. Things have a way of self-correcting. It's more of an ethical issue than a temporal one, really."

Helen eyes the console full of gadgetry behind Wally. She toys with the idea of shooting the machinery to pieces. The shotgun is loaded, and the anger in her heart has several times pushed hard enough to break something since she walked into the cave. Still, she discards the plan as quickly as it came to her.

"Helen, if you tell me it's what you want, I promise you personally that we will leave tomorrow, as soon as we can shut everything down," says Arnold. "And that neither of us, nor anyone else from our company, will ever come back to bother you. All I would need is for you to sign a non-disclosure form."

Helen considers this.

"I appreciate that, Arnold. I do. But it occurs to me that this situation, it's as much my fault as it is yours and Wally's."

Helen stands up, picking the gun up with her. Looking from Arnold to Wally, she leaves it hovering. "I'm not sure what to think right now, gentlemen. So, I'd like to sleep on it, if I can," she says.

"Of course," says Arnold.

"Absolutely," says Wally.

Helen and Omega walk home through the yarrow and the waving grass, the sound of the creek babbling behind them. Helen's sense of calm has returned.

As they come up on the house, Helen asks Omega "What do you think, girl? Would you trust them?" Omega wags her tail and pants before sitting down by the garden fence.

Helen eats her dinner alone and starts reading *Flight of Whimsy*. At nine o'clock, she calls an old friend of John's and asks him for two favours. Then she calls Arnold and invites him and Wally to come by the next morning for a late breakfast.

The men arrive in awkward silence. Arnold takes off his hat and holds it over his heart, as if he's in a John Wayne western or at a funeral.

"Come in," says Helen through the screen door.

"I've been doing a lot of thinking since yesterday," she says as they come into the kitchen. "Actually, truth be told, I guess it's been for a lot longer than that." She serves the omelettes onto their plates and sets a plate stacked with crisp bacon in the middle of the table.

"Did you know I had planned to travel the world? Before John, I mean?" She sets out the basket of fresh, warm bread. "It's something he said he loved about me when we met. He said he wanted to join me. Our trip to New York was supposed to be just the start. We were going to travel all through the United Stated, Mexico, Europe. I even thought maybe India." Helen pours Arnold and Wally their coffees. Both men are standing behind their chairs, appearing unsure of whether to sit while Helen still bustles around them.

"But then we moved here, and we made different choices. For a long time, I blamed him. I felt it was all his fault—my lost opportunities, me giving up my dreams. But I made those choices." She adds a bowl of mixed berries and cream to the breakfast display, then takes her spot at the head of the table.

"You see," she says, unfolding the napkin neatly onto the lap of her skirt, "I decided to choose him. To choose here. To be with the wildflowers and the man I loved."

Arnold and Wally each pull out their chair. They pass each other a quick, questioning look and pause a moment before finally sitting down.

"I've been wondering lately if maybe John would have been willing to make different choices, with me, if I had made my case more plainly at the time, shown him how important my dreams were to me."

None of the three have begun to eat, although Arnold has started to sip at his coffee.

"The funny thing is, I see this—what you two have done— it's the same thing," says Helen. She leans in toward the men, lowers her voice for emphasis. Her nerves have been bothering her since she got up this morning, but she has pushed on with each step of her plan so far, and she does not want to stop. "What you two have done to me is what I've done to myself. I'm a 52-year-old, educated woman, and I have willingly let you turn me into a gullible, doddering idiot baking bread to, presumably, make you rich. I must have made you quite a lot of money by now, I imagine."

It's a question aimed at Arnold.

"It was a slow start," he says. "But yeah, the last year has been very good. We're starting to get... well, bidding wars."

Helen hushes the flutter of anger in her heart.

"I can see why," she says. "It must have been very charming for your guests to see the stupid lady from the past who has no idea what's going on."

"Helen!" both Wally and Arnold start, the word in stereo a sinuous whine.

"It wasn't like that," Arnold tries. "We never made a fool out of you in any way."

"I made sure all the guests would only have the utmost respect for you," says Wally. "It was a key part of the agreement."

Wally lowers his gaze to the table.

"You must know, Helen, that I care for you very much," he nearly whispers. "I would never let them make a fool of you."

Helen breathes deeply and straightens her back to steel herself against her instincts toward the Wally she'd come to have feelings for. The idea of her plan is easier than the execution. Last night, she demonized Wally and Arnold until they no longer resembled her friends at all, but today her old Wally and Arnold have come to breakfast. They look guilty and conciliatory, but they still feel like her friends.

"I can't imagine the kind of future you live in," Helen continues, "but I'm certain it was created by people exactly like you. People who didn't realize, or didn't want to realize, the repercussions of their actions. I'm sorry for you," she says, nodding to Arnold and then Wally, to show them her pity is honest. "And I'm sorry for all those young people who came here, if this was their escape from something awful. I don't blame them for coming. But I do blame you both. I have to. And me. The more I think about it, the more it seems all three of us have been using my situation to validate our own means." A deep sigh escapes Helen's lips. She looks from one man to the other. The morning light proves the furrows of worry and age on both their faces.

A loud bang resonates in the distance, followed by the sound of Omega barking frantically from within the garden fence. Wally and Arnold pivot to look out the kitchen window.

"What was that?" asks Wally, standing to see better. Checkered yellow curtains frame a cloud of dirt billowing in the distance, creating a mushroom beyond the nearest hills.

"Your machine," says Helen. Her words sound calm, but her heart is beating faster, unsure of Wally and Arnold's reactions. "I called an old blasting friend of John's last night and asked him for some explosives to blow up a troublesome beaver damn."

"What have you done to us?" asks Arnold, staring out the window.

"Don't be so dramatic," says Helen. "Everyone sit. Have your breakfast."

Wally and Arnold watch Helen as she finally starts, as calmly as she is able, to eat her breakfast. Eventually, they join her, and the three eat in silence.

"More bacon?" asks Helen when her guests are nearly done their plates.

Silence.

"Okay, then," she says. She takes another slice for herself. She eats it slowly, then dabs her napkin to the corners of her mouth. The weight of the two men's emotions is beginning to sit heavily at the table. Helen feels a glimmer of remorse.

"It's not about revenge," she says, "if that's what you're thinking." She is careful to make eye contact with both of them. "Although, I admit I thought it would feel good to take away your control over your futures the way you did to me. But, Arnold, you said there are a few other companies such as yours, am I right?"

"Yes," he says, solemnly.

"So you can find a way home, if you want?"

"I suppose, yeah. The nearest one's in Europe. I wouldn't be quite sure how to reach them. It's a whole other business, and they just started up. But I figure we could find it, in a pinch."

Wally looks toward Arnold, but Helen cannot read the expression on Wally's face.

"Wally also said, though, that you've both spent more time here than you originally planned to."

"Yes," says Arnold.

"Well, I was thinking that, if you wanted, you could keep the Bed and Breakfast."

"What do you mean?" asks Arnold.

"Well, you have your horses here, and Wally already knows the business. If you'd like to run it—in this time, I mean—you can."

"But, what about you?" asks Wally.

"Oh, you wouldn't get me. I would be a silent partner. From afar. I would take forty per cent of the net, leaving you each with 30 and lodgings, if you want them. I would also need you to care for Omega—and your horses of course, Arnold—while I'm gone."

"Gone?" asks Wally. Gone where? The wrinkles on his forehead have sunk even deeper with concern. Helen notices the fine, grey stubble on his cheeks and jaw. His blue eyes are pale and watery. He looks derelict. Helen wonders what she saw in him. Maybe it was only proximity that made her heart grow fond.

Still, she feels sorry for him.

"Away," she answers. "I've decided to do some travelling of my own again, at last. I have the money. And the time. And now, thanks to you, I have the push I needed."

From the lot comes the sound of a truck pulling in. John's old friend, Reg, has come to take her to the city.

"I'm going to freshen up. When I come back, could you help me with my bags, please, gentlemen?" she asks Arnold and Wally.

Helen leaves Arnold and Wally in the living room. She scans her room for anything she may have forgotten to pack. Downstairs, she hears the rough mutters of an impromptu meeting between boss and wayward employee. Their voices grumble back and forth from the base of the stairs.

"Have you decided what to do?" Helen asks as she comes down, her hat and purse in hand.

"Wally's going to stay," says Arnold. Wally nods to Helen. "But I'm going to try to head back."

They load Helen's two suitcases into the back of Reg's red Ford. Arnold closes the tailgate. He draws Helen gently around to the side of the truck. His voice is low.

"I want you to know, Helen, that I understand what you did," he says, his hand still on her forearm. "And I also just want you to know again that we're really sorry—that I'm really sorry."

"I know, Arnold," she says, putting her sunhat on. Then she adds, "Say, could you promise me something?"

"Of course."

"Could you fix the barbecue for Wally before you go?"

Arnold's face crumples with disappointment. He releases Helen's arm and looks down toward his cowboy boots. They are dusted with fresh dirt from the gravel lane.

"And could you also give him whatever business advice you can? He'll need to hire a cook, too. I left a list of possible candidates, and the name and number of the local bakery. It's all on the kitchen counter. It will eat into his profits, though, so anything you can do to help would be good."

"Of course," says Arnold. His lips are drawn in a tight line. She knows he is feeling rebuffed. She wishes she could give him more, give him the same freedom she feels now that she is finally learning to let go.

"Arnold?" she asks.

"Yes?"

"Is it really that bad in your time?"

Arnold looks out to the hills. The dust of the explosion has long settled. Above the mountains hangs only a thin puff of white clouds.

"It's better here," he says. "It's definitely better here."

"Can you promise me one more thing then, Arnold?"

"Of course."

"Take your time going home. See the world. I plan to. I hear it's still rather nice to see."

Arnold looks at her. Confusion clouds his sun-worn face. Then his smile grows bright and warm, his crow's-feet spreading across his tanned skin. He sees the gift Helen is offering him. She knows he recognizes it for what it is.

"Thank you," he says. "I think I might just do that."

He kisses her lightly on her forehead, then nods his goodbye, his cowboy hat back on his head.

As Arnold walks away toward the house, Helen motions Wally over. Reg is waiting patiently in the truck. He was always such a good friend to John. She reminds herself to send him and his wife something from her travels, to thank him for responding so quickly and kindly to her sudden, strange requests.

"Wally," Helen says softly, as he nears.

"Helen," he answers. He can't quite meet her eyes, his gaze stalling somewhere around the spot Arnold just kissed, although she guesses his choice is not conscious.

"Wally, I'm not mad," she says. "I need you to know that. I thought about it all night, and if I can forgive myself, I can forgive you. But I want you to do something for me."

"What is it?" he asks, as hopeful as Arnold was.

Helen pauses. This is the trump she was waiting to play, her gift to Wally. She doesn't want it to seem manipulative, or to sound trite.

"Don't let Arnold go see the damage before he leaves," she says.

She has leaned in close to make sure Arnold can't hear, even though he's already too far to hear anything quieter than a holler.

Helen sees the old light in Wally's eyes as they twinkle with suspicion.

"Why?" he asks her, head tilted in anticipation.

"Just make sure he doesn't see it," she says. "Then go see for yourself once he's gone."

A smile of understanding spreads across Wally's face.

"Helen..." he whispers.

"I've just started thinking lately that everyone should be in control of their own destiny," says Helen. "Even if they need a helping push to take it."

Wally wraps his arms around Helen, squeezing tight before releasing her.

"Thank you," he whispers. "And have a great adventure, Helen."

"I will," she whispers back. "I absolutely will."

As Reg drives her down the lane toward the highway, Helen looks to the two men watching her from the front step of her and John's old home. She wishes them both truly well. As Omega barks her goodbye from the garden, Helen breathes in the smell of the summer grass and the honeysuckle.

She pulls out her atlas to plan the first leg of her trip. She'll start small, then see what happens.

Terrarium

The day after the earthquake, Kirsten's turtle died.

The turtle, a small, dark green thing about the size of Kirsten's outspread hand, had been trying to escape ever since Kirsten had moved the two of them to the city four months earlier. Bit would push himself up the glass wall of the terrarium with his front legs until he was upright, his pale yellow underbelly pressed against the clear glass, his foreclaws grasping toward whatever he dreamed might offer him a foothold to climb his way to freedom. After work, Kirsten would come home to find him lying on his back, his legs slowly treading the air in a noiseless plea to be righted.

The day Bit died, Kirsten came home and found him lying on his back. She clicked the light on above the hall table and reached in to turn him over, but his head and legs stayed tucked inside his shell. Kirsten put him down gently in the middle of the terrarium, on a small plain of sand between two patches of plastic grass, and watched him for a while. After dinner, Kirsten came back to see if anything had changed. She called her veterinarian's emergency number and explained what was wrong. She prodded the turtle as he suggested. Nothing happened.

"I'm sorry, Kirsten. It sounds like your turtle has died."

Bit wasn't the first resident of the little terrarium, but Kirsten had had high hopes for him. She had read somewhere that there were sea turtles who lived to be more than 200 years old. Kirsten was sure pet store turtles didn't live as long as that, but she decided they must live a good number of years, and she bought herself one. Kirsten lifted the lid to the dumpster in the alley beside her apartment building and lowered Bit gently into the soft crevice between two large, black garbage bags.

The next day, Kirsten's mourning clothes, from grey Mary Janes to a black pashmina her mother had given her years earlier, blended in with the sullenness that had settled over the city since the quake. It was being referred to in the news as "a likely precursor to the big one." It had knocked out part of a freeway, toppled several older bridges, and brought down the roof of a small, but surprisingly busy, shopping mall.

The quake shredded a jagged line up the coast and south through a row of coastal towns and suburbs, to the city centre. Kirsten watched the estimated death toll rise and fall and rise again on up-to-the-minute newscasts ever since she and everyone else in the IT office came out from under their desks and drew straight to the boardroom TV.

Since the shaking stopped, Kirsten, who had always been nervous at the calmest of times, felt like it hadn't quit at all. She started having nightmares that she had been responsible for the earthquake, for the existence of the fault line itself, that the whole planet would explode or disappear if she did the wrong thing: picked up the wrong pen, got on the wrong train, bought the wrong brand of toothpaste. She would wake up terrified, desperate to remember what the latest wrong thing had been, careful not to make the same mistake in real life.

Kirsten felt as if the ricochet between ground and people had moved inside of her instead of stopping. Standing in front of her bathroom mirror the morning after, she became too aware of her breathing. She couldn't think of anything but the next inhalation, the next movement of air. She felt like maybe, if she breathed the wrong breath at the wrong moment, she might trigger something—something big, something awful. Like another quake. Or something bigger.

The feeling stayed with her all morning. Everything amplified. She had forgotten about her breaths at some point while eating her cereal. But, by the time she got outside, she was elaborately conscious of every step. Her feet weighed heavy in her shoes, seemed to make more noise against the ground than everyone else's. What if she stepped on the wrong piece of concrete, touched the toe of her sneaker to the wrong crack, and, just like that, ended everything, blew it all away in chaotic explosion, or snuffed it out like a candle?

Four days earlier, anyone would have thought she was paranoid, delusional with fear and exacerbation as she walked the narrow, downtown sidewalks to work. Today, if she told someone what was in her head, she was certain what they would think: *Poor thing. These things affect us all differently. You're not the only one.* It made her feel normal. This was to be expected.

"What if the whole Earth was booby trapped and someone's just waiting for us to set it off?" Kirsten asked in the cafeteria. She was sitting across from John, the only person who regularly had lunch with her. They would both get caught up in their work and forget to have lunch until everyone else was already done.

"What if the trigger was something crazy, something everyday, obvious? Like a kid playing on the sidewalk? Or this sandwich?" she continued.

John looked at Kirsten's egg salad sandwich, its thick web of mayonnaise binding two slices of white bread. John looked back at Kirsten and didn't say anything.

She could see in the intent way he was studying her that she was making him uncomfortable. He probably wanted to tell her "You're crazy" or "Stop being paranoid" or "Shut up," but Kirsten knew he was too polite.

Or maybe, she thought, maybe he thinks I'm right.

"My turtle died," she said instead, then bit into her sandwich. Her comment received the sympathetic look she had expected.

"Oh, I'm sorry. How long had you had him?" John pushed the dried crust of his own sandwich to the corner of his tray.

"Two years." Another bite. Kirsten became aware of her chewing, the food moving deliberately in her mouth with the motion of jaws and tongue, grinding and sliding, wet and repetitive. What was the right amount, the number of chews a person should chew? She'd heard a nutritionist say on a talk show, years ago. What was it?

"Oh," said John. The space around Kirsten became heavier again. John would need time to think of something else to say now. It's a good question, she thought, swallowing. She took another bite of her sandwich. Obviously, this wasn't the trigger. She remembered a lot of people asking her that when Eli left last year.

"I'm sorry to hear about you and Eli," they would say. "How long had you two been together?"

It gives people a good gage for knowing how sorry they should look, she thought.

In the pet store, Kirsten ran her fingers along the panes of some of the dozens of aquariums and terrariums. She stopped to look at two rabbits. One was lying on the other's head, a long, black ear hanging down to cover its sibling's face. Their two bodies breathed big and slow and heavy together.

Kirsten chose a gecko. The little lizard clung, phosphorescent and sleek, to the side of its glass box. He looked healthy. She tapped on the glass, and he darted across it, clambering over two bigger, less energetic lizards along the way. She named him Dart.

In the hallway, Kirsten turned the light on over the terrarium. She took Dart out of his small, plastic case and placed him on the back of her left hand. He looked up at her as she stroked him gently from his head to his tail with her index finger.

Kirsten lifted the lid from the terrarium with one hand and slid it behind the glass cage, against the wall. She petted Dart's brilliant, light green skin some more. Kirsten marveled at how he seemed to be making eye contact with her.

"It's just so you won't run off," she whispered. She picked him gently from the back of her hand and set him on the patch of sand where her turtle had been the night before.

Kirsten kept stroking the bright little gecko as she picked up one of the larger rocks from the mound in the corner of the miniature world. She rolled the stone's rough shape between her fingers. The gecko started to squirm. Kirsten pinned him down on the sand by the skin of his sides. She pressed the rock onto the stretch of spine between Dart's front legs, pushing gradually harder until she felt a small snap, and Dart stopped moving.

Kirsten put the rock back on the pile, slid the lid back onto the terrarium, and headed to the living room for the evening news.

Anita Dolman

A Few Times a Year

A few times a year, Lana finds herself overcome by a feeling that something amazing and unexpected is just about to happen. She wakes up in an inexplicably cheerful mood, and the feeling wells inside of her all morning.

Things that were boring the day before are newly exotic and full of potential, filling her with a constant sense of "Anything could happen next." Taking an order for 5,000 plastic bags at the manufacturing company where she works seems suddenly momentous and leads to all manner of thrilling questions.

"What if this were the last order I ever took?"

"What's going to end up in all those bags?"

"What if someone uses one to dump a body? Whose would it be? Would they get caught?"

Lana can picture a man dragging a giant bag to the edge of a dark river in the night. He's under a bridge. The police are on their way. The body hits the water. He's making his getaway. The rocks are slippery. The sirens are approaching.

Normally, by noon, when Lana is eating her pressed chicken sandwich, she starts thinking about what it means that she did not win the $50,000 promised by the scratch ticket she bought on her coffee break, or that she was not abducted on her way back to work, or that the police still have not called to inquire about a bag sold some time ago to a suspicious gentleman. Lana then starts to get an equally swelling feeling that she is going to have to take matters into her own hands.

It is in these moments Lana becomes, in her husband's word, *dangerous*.

When she gets this feeling, Lana usually gives Fred fair warning. She'll call him at his office at the chicken factory and say something like "I just know something amazing is going to happen."

Statements like these have, in the past, led Fred to increase their insurance, call their investment advisor, or find a way to need to leave, immediately, and with almost no warning, on a business trip.

This is because Fred has learned that any lunchtime phone call beginning with Lana saying "I just know…" is a guaranteed sign there will be a dinnertime announcement along the line of "What do you think of hot-air ballooning?" or "I've really been thinking about it, and I don't know why we stopped at two kids."

Last year, it led to Fred's least favourite dinner pronouncement yet: "I'm thinking reno."

Twenty-thousand dollars later, and the loss of the only remotely masculine room that had been left in their house in the first place—now called the "powder room"—meant that yesterday at lunch when Lana called Fred at work and said, "I can feel it. It's going to be something major," Fred was terrified.

It also meant that, after two decades of Lana's announcements, he was finally ready.

Ten thousand feet above sea level, and 125 feet from the top of Vulcan Mountain in the Sierra Madre range of Wyoming is a little rock jut just big enough to sit on, next to which a little waterfall no wider than the length of an arm tumbles quietly and endlessly into the narrow creek weaving through the valley below.

It is here that Lana, attached to nearly 100 feet of rope and clamped into her bright orange rock-climbing boots with matching helmet, is taking a momentary break, despite the guide continuing to call her from above to keep going, to climb up, up, up to the inevitable blue sky sprawled out above the top of the mountain that has become her nemesis.

And it is here that Lana, thinking it over now, is coming to the conclusion that this is really not what she had had in mind when she came home three weeks ago with a plan for a change.

Her change, after all, was going to be to the kitchen. In fact, the specific change she had intended that day would have looked quite a lot like page 28 of the May edition of her favourite home magazine.

But when Lana got to the front door that Tuesday, Fred was already home. Fred, who came home at 5:13 p.m. every, single day, had opened the door for Lana at exactly 4:45 as she was coming up the walk. Lana noticed him as he was quickly ducking his hands behind his back, a peculiar shine in his blue eyes.

"I've been thinking..." he started as she got to the stoop. The mischievous grin on his face was one that, come to think of it, she hadn't seen in a very long time.

"About what?" she asked hesitantly. It was then Lana had started to feel a slightly sinking sensation, just a kind of light tingle all through her body, telling her that something, somehow, was going slightly askew in her world.

The feeling had not left since.

So, today, 10,000 feet above sea level, and 125 feet from the top of Vulcan Mountain in the Sierra Madre range of Wyoming, Lana MacDonald is sitting on a tiny precipice of rock, of a deep gray colour not entirely unlike that she had been envisioning for her new slate countertops when, home magazines in hand, she had been greeted by her husband at the front door of their duplex.

One thing Lana had always been certain of about Fred was he knew what he wanted, and he knew what he didn't. He definitely did not want more kids, and he won there; and he definitely did not want to go hot-air balloon into the setting sun, and he won there, although Lana did go with a friend, and he didn't really want the new bathroom and hallway, although he gave in there, bless his heart.

Anita Dolman

But something Lana had never known about her husband in 23 years of marriage was a thing he really did want. Fred MacDonald really wanted to climb Mount Vulcan.

And he didn't just want to climb it. He had read about Mount Vulcan in an issue of *Reader's Digest* his dad had shown him when he was 12 years old. His dad had thought it was kind of funny, with Fred being so into Star Trek and all, and, from there, the idea had stuck. And grown. Fred had planned to do it with some friends after high school. But then one of them got sick, and Fred got a summer job at the factory, and it never happened the way things don't.

When Lana called three weeks ago, Fred finally saw his opportunity. And he took it.

He's coming up now, about 20 feet below Lana—his pointy ears wobbling from the heat and the sweat, the perfectly straight bangs of his Spock haircut starting to look a little less Vulcan and a little more messy, and his silver communicator glistening in the sun against the backdrop of his blue, polyester uniform.

Lana had at least gotten him to agree to let her wear bike shorts under the tiny, orange Uhura skirt, but it seems a small victory now. Her arms and legs feel ready to fall off, her hands feel like they've been peeled open from clutching onto the tall grass and then the boulders and now the increasingly steep rock dotted with the metal pins placed so helpfully by their guide for their "security." And there are still another 125 painfully steep feet to go before they reach the top.

"How you doing, babe?" Fred calls up. He's almost at the ledge now, which means she should get moving. "You still hanging in there?"

Lana manages a sarcastic smile, scrunching her nose up at him. "You know, this really isn't what I'd had in mind," she says. "It may have been your turn, and I totally agree that that's fair, but I still say you're going to owe me for this. I never once asked you to dress up in anything other than a suit."

Fred looks up at her. He's just a few feet from the ledge. He looks happy. Really happy. For a moment they just smile at each other.

"I'm thinking next time we come up with something together," says Lana, as she dusts her skirt off and hauls herself back into position. There was a stack of travel magazines in the breakfast nook of their hotel. She's thinking of suggesting Paris for their anniversary.

"Actually, I've been thinking about that," says Fred. "And I figure I'm still a few behind with ideas."

Anita Dolman

Alumni Magazine, Classified Ad

I'm writing to tell you I've been named accountability manager at the region's third-largest performance estimation firm. In 1995, I married my fellow alum, Sue. We went to Hawaii for our honeymoon. I haven't gone anywhere since. Oh, God. I miss sunsets from the library roof, getting stoned with Dave and Keith. Life just keeps getting smaller now. Keith killed himself last fall. I haven't heard from Dave since graduation. He didn't come to the funeral. If anyone knows where he is...

We have two adorable children, Danny and Lori. I wanted more, but Sue had a miscarriage and a hysterectomy. We finally sold the crib in a garage sale last June. I think she hates me. We still have sex every Thursday, but it's not the same. We own a beautiful house, with two acres and a pool. Sue was fired from the hospital last month when she showed up drunk again. Now she just sleeps. I want to tell you I've done my best to use my sociology degree, but there were so many bills, and everyone has to work somewhere.

My hobbies are raising goldfish and watching gay porn with my neighbour, Steve. Although I don't let him do anything to me. Much. I don't paint anymore, and I haven't skied since the accident. Some days, I think about packing the car and leaving. Maybe heading south. Maybe with Steve. I'm writing to tell you I have disappeared. I'm writing in case you remember me.

Anita Dolman

Rabbit

Cory races across six lawns to tell his sister Rose what's happened.

"He's been bit! Jeffie's been bit."

"Bit? By what?" Rose is watering the lawn.

"Mr. Parkinson's retriever."

"Whistle?"

"Yeah!"

"You sure?"

"There's blood."

"Okay. I'm coming." Rose turns the gage. She overshoots "Off" and "Sprinkle," spraying water into her new leather sandals. Cory had better not be making up another story. Last week, Rose spent half an hour looking for the backpack he said had rolled down Demon Hill before he admitted he'd accidentally left it at school.

Cory races ahead, back to Rose, ahead again in impatience, his bright red T-shirt making him seem to her like a small stop sign constantly being moved by pranksters up and down the street.

"It's probably just a scratch," she calls after him.

Rounding the corner to the Roberts', Rose sees right away that Cory isn't lying. Jeffie is crumpled on the lawn like a broken accordion. Toys are scattered all around him.

Rose pushes into a run, promptly loses a sandal in an edging of weeds. She launches across the grass to the eight-year-old.

"Cory! Go call 911!"

Jeffie is pale as lightning. His jean shorts, his Angry Birds T-shirt, everything is soaked in blood. His breathing is slow and shallow. His eyes are closed.

"Cory!"

Mrs. Evenstein pulls into her drive across the street.

"Mrs. Evenstein!" Rose shouts as the old woman emerges from her car. "Call 911! Right away! Jeffie's been bitten. He needs an ambulance—immediately!"

Mrs. Evenstein races to her door, drops her keys on the mat, picks them up again, disappears into the bungalow.

Rose brushes a tangle of bangs from the boy's forehead. She thinks his skin feels cold.

"It's going to be okay," she whispers, not at all sure.

She remembers Cory and looks up. It feels like hours before he comes back around the corner. She notices his white sneakers are smeared with red. His pace slows as he comes closer.

"Where is Jeffie's mom?" Rose asks.

"Shopping," Cory answers, his eyes fixed on Jeffie.

Rose starts to feel around for the wound, slides her fingers under Jeffie's body. They slip straight into flesh beneath his bottom rib. Her fingers recoil, slick with red and yellow. Seeing them, she spins away hard, still on her knees, then vomits onto the grass.

She forces herself to breathe, to recover, to think. She thinks "Look up."

Rose sees Whistle laying dead in the flowerbed in front of her, his eyes like yellow marbles. A bloody baseball bat tossed behind him. A rabbit gnawed nearly in two between him and the boy.

Rose turns to Cory, who is trapped, frozen, at the edge of the lawn.

"What did you do?"

Rose imagines she can hear the first sirens echoing in the distance.

"It's not my fault," says Cory, his eyes on Whistle... Jeffie... Rose. "We caught a rabbit. Whistle wanted it. It was just a game. It's not my fault."

Anita Dolman

The Drop-Offs

Green; amber; red. Henri's nights slide by beneath the stop-and-go of traffic lights.

Another Friday night, same as the one before, except for the rain blurring the city's colours through the windshield. The clock on the dashboard reads 9:15, which means Ms. Winchester in front of the Royal Ontario Museum. Henri doesn't know where she really lives, or where she works, and he has never for a moment believed her name is Ms. Winchester. The tail of her tailored, navy pea coat flutters behind her in the wet breeze as Henri opens the rear door for her. She slides onto the leather seat, drawing the high-heels of her designer pumps in with an educated grace.

Whoever she is, Henri imagines she will have told her husband, once again, that she had to return to the office after the kids were in bed, will have reminded him, if he was still listening, that she needs to put in the extra hours required from any woman who has dented, but not yet broken through, the glass ceiling.

9:20 and Ms. Winchester's *garçon*, as Henri thinks of him, is waiting at the usual coffee shop on Bloor Street. His thick, black hair has just the right amount of gel to make it look naturally unruly. He often shows up carrying his guitar—a worn, wooden acoustic with a beautiful, curved top board. *God only knows how these two ever met*, Henri thought the first time he picked them up, in the same order, two months ago.

The drop-off at the hotel comes around 9:30, and then Henri won't see them again for at least two hours, when

Ms. Winchester will call his cell to ask that he bring the car around front.

The luxury car service for which Henri works can bill either by the hour or the pick-up. Ms. Winchester always pays for the entire evening. Henri thinks of this as the only wise move she is making in the entire affair: always leaving herself the option of escape at any point. The rest of her decisions are beyond Henri's attempts to understand. How, for example, can she be so careful to avoid being recognized during pick-ups and drop-offs yet, after her rendezvous, walk her lanky, aspiring Elvis proudly out through the lobby of a popular hotel, clasped to his arm like a proud bride?

A moment from Henri's wedding day plays in his mind as he slows for a red: Agnes's hair twined with small, white flowers. The soft, fragile feel of her hand in his as they walked back up the aisle together, married for the rest of their lives.

Henri focuses on the rear-view mirror to supplant the memory.

Garçon is leaning in close to Ms. Winchester, his hand resting on top of hers. A streetlight casts his face half in shadow, half in soft, yellow light.

The car behind Henri honks a polite prompt. Henri slides his foot to the gas, his gaze back to the street ahead.

People count too much on others not noticing their secrets, not recognizing who they really are behind the show they've put on, thinks Henri. Or perhaps Ms. Winchester's husband already knows what she is doing. Perhaps everyone in her life is aware of exactly who and what she is. Possibly she is the only person she is still fooling.

Henri drops the peculiar couple off in front of the hotel, then parks the car. He tries to let the idea of them go, as well. He normally tries not to think a lot about his clients. Henri collects his paperback from the glove box—another Scottish mystery, this one a strangling in the moors. He heads to the deli across the street. Henri and one of his favourite detectives. A distant tragedy. And a piece of apple pie with cheese.

"Another Scottish mystery?" asks Sarah as she pours Henri's coffee.

"You ne'er saw me," he winks. He suspects his fake accent makes him sound more like a B-list Muppet than an actual Scotsman, but Sarah, as usual, repays his foolishness with a kind smile.

"I will nae' tell a soul," she says before heading back to her counter.

Sarah's eyes are chocolate brown and patient. Her skin colour is different than Henri's, and she must already be about 20 years old, but, knowing the caring way she treats her customers, Henri nonetheless thinks yet again, *This is what my daughter would have been like.*

There is a picture in Henri's wallet from the six-month ultrasound, four days before the aneurism. *Before Agnes died of an aneurism*, he thinks. Henri is supposed to practice saying the words, to help him come to terms with it. According to the book his doctor recommended, he is supposed to say them out loud, to another person. But there is no one in his life to say them to.

"Agnes' aneurism," he whispers to his coffee. He doesn't feel any different. He doesn't feel anything. Henri checks his watch. Ms. Winchester won't call for at least another hour and a half. He opens his paperback again.

"Henri, how are we going to help you get a handle on this?" his doctor asked last year.

"It's just the job. I can't get used to working nights."

"Henri, it's been nearly a year since Agnes died."

"Agnes and the baby."

"Agnes and the baby," repeated Dr. Bingham.

"I just need a refill on the sleeping pills, please."

"Henri, the pscyh referral I wrote you last year will have run out by now, so I'm going to write you another one. I want you to go. Dr. Broadbent is an excellent psychologist. I think she can really help you."

"I just need some sleep."

"Henri, you're a smart man. Please see Dr. Broadbent. You need to let someone in."

"I just need sleep."

"At least read the book I recommended."

"I will. I promise."

The deli is quiet. Sarah is talking with a table of three art students near the front. One of them, a young red-head, has a tattoo on her left shoulder, of a baby cradled in a rose blossom.

Agnes had a younger brother who died of leukemia when she was seven. She had his birth sign, Aquarius, and his name—Andrew—tattooed on the small of her back.

"If I'd known I'd never be able to get an epidural because of it, I would have gotten it on my shoulder instead," she told Henri on their way home from their doctor.

"You're not going to need it, anyway," Henri said. "The baby will come quick and easy. No problem at all."

Agnes arched an eyebrow.

"It could happen," said Henri.

She arched it higher.

"It will happen," he said, kissing her on the top of her head. "You'll see. It will be fine."

"More coffee?"

Sarah has snuck up on Henri. He wonders how long he has been staring at the same page without reading. He checks his watch. There is still at least another hour until the call.

"Yes, please," he says, raising the scratched, ceramic mug for Sarah to fill.

"Book not all you hoped for?" asks Sarah. Her observation skills continue to impress Henri. At times, he worries she sees more about him than he wants her to.

"It's alright," he says. "I'm just easily distracted, I suppose."

Sarah tilts her head. Agnes used to make the same gesture when deep in thought.

"Can I ask you something?" Henri notices Sarah is rocking lightly back and forth on her heels as she speaks. "And please feel totally free to say 'No.' I won't be hurt or anything. I have no business asking, really, since you're a customer, and since we barely know each other."

Henri can't imagine what she could want to ask him. His heart starts to beat faster. He wants to leave, to pay his bill and go, but he doesn't.

"You can always ask," he says instead, surprising himself with the calm and reasoned sound of his words. "If I do not want to answer, we can always go back to coffee and Scottish detectives."

Sarah scans the restaurant. The art students are all well into their meals, and she already served or topped up the few regulars at the counter on her way to Henri.

"Hold on a sec'," she says. "I'm just going to put the coffeepot back."

Watching her return to him, Henri notices her outfit. Her dress is straight from the 1950s, with cap sleeves and a tea-length skirt swinging along over a crinoline petticoat. The creamy cotton of the dress is patterned with a toile of finely drawn, blue roosters and farm houses. Sarah has a flare for the artistic and the ironic. Henri wonders again if this is what his daughter would have been like. *Or would she have been entirely different? Maybe a soccer player, with a jersey and a ponytail?*

"Mind if I sit down?" asks Sarah.

"Of course not," says Henri. He opens his palm toward the opposite bench.

"Thanks," says Sarah, sliding onto the red vinyl. "So, I know it's none of my business," she starts.

Henri's heart feels suspended.

"But you're, like, a limo driver, right?"

"Of a sort. I drive for a luxury car service."

"Oh."

Henri decides not to bore her with the difference.

"Well," she continues, "I was wondering if you would be interested in helping me with this, um, project I started."

Sarah explains that her night shift ends at the same time the new pastries are delivered. So, early each morning, she gathers all of the unsold Danishes and muffins and coffee cake and other treats into a box and takes them to the mission, about 15 blocks away.

"There was a guy who worked here for a while. He had a car, and so he helped me take it all over every morning. But he quit last week to go out west."

"And so your not-for profit would like to hire my car service?" Henri smiles.

"Very funny." Sarah scrunches her nose up into a little accordion.

"What time is the drop-off?"

"Six a.m."

Henri looks out the picture window but only sees the bright reflection of the deli's interior shining back at him. He sees himself, sitting across from Sarah. He sees her watching him, expectant, while he considers the world of Formica and bright chrome she inhabits nearly every night. *A young woman in the city should know better*, he thinks. Detective novels and a steady job or not, I could easily be any type of man. She should be more careful.

"I know it's late," says Sarah.

"I do not mind that part," he says, looking back to her. I should not have said it like that, he thinks. What part will she now suppose I do mind? Her? Helping the poor?

Henri notices the motion of Sarah's hands in her lap. She has wrapped her tea towel around the fingers of her left hand. She unwinds it, then promptly coils it around her fingers again without looking.

"Okay," she says. "Well, promise you'll think about it?" She starts to slide out of the booth.

"It's a very nice thing you are doing," Henri says, surprising himself. "And it's a good idea of yours—wise and thoughtful."

"So you'll think about it?"

"I promise I will consider it very seriously."

"Good," she says. "Thank you."

The opening and closing of the glass double doors soon draws Henri back up from his detective's slow progress. The aging sleuth is still standing on the moor, still surveying the crime-festooned riverbed below. Exactly as he has been all evening.

Ms. Winchester's young man is looking around the deli. Henri searches his memory for the name the young man gave him the first night Henri picked them up. David, perhaps? Marcus?

Henri normally considers it good business to avoid knowing exactly these kinds of details. But now he regrets letting the young man's name drift away so easily, even if it was only a pseudonym, too.

The *garçon* spots Henri and heads toward his booth. He is lightly bouncing his shoulders inside his leather jacket to warm himself. Henri sees him scan the turntable of pies and tarts by the counter, before focussing again on his goal.

"It's Henri, right?" he asks. Under the florescent light, his hair looks even blacker, and his eyes as pale as morning sky. He holds his hand out to the chauffeur, as if they had not seen each other only an hour before.

Henri envelopes the hand in front of him. It is dry and surprisingly warm. *He must have stuffed his hands into his pockets for the dash across the street*, thinks Henri.

"I'm—"

"No," says Henri. "Better not to tell me. Plausible deniability can be useful in my line of work."

"Yeah." The young man grins, then looks down at his battered, black running shoes. "I guess it would be." He sits in Sarah's spot. "But anyway, it's Justin."

Henri looks toward the door, then back to Justin.

"Should you not be with your... client?" Henri asks.

The young man's full smile is open and disarming, his teeth a stark white. He has no scent about him, Henri realizes. His clothes are those of a young man living in his time. But they are clean and neat. Henri had, until now, purposely tried not to look too closely at either the young man or his customer. Nonetheless, he had assumed that a prostitute of any kind, even a young one, would be wearing some outward sign of hard luck.

"Well, good sir, my client, as you call her, is, in polite terms, thoroughly passed out in her overpriced, king-sized bed."

"I'm sorry. It's not my business."

"That's alright." But Justin's voice has flattened from its earlier deep melody of welcoming tones. He looks away, toward the row of plastic-coated menus tucked between the salt and pepper shakers and the window ledge. He pulls one out from the middle and turns to the burgers page.

"It's not the way you think," he says, still looking at the menu. "Well, it is, but... it's not as seedy as that, I mean."

"I don't wish to judge," says Henri. "Everyone's life is their own." He feels compelled to offer the boy some kind of assurance. "I am in no position to criticize anyone's choices." He closes his eyes for a moment to block out the fluorescent lights above, and the past two years. "No one is."

"Yeah, I know." Justin looks up.

Henri opens his eyes. He takes in the young man's expression. Henri recognizes the isolated desperation in his eyes. Justin leans forward.

"I want you to know that I'm not a whore, though," he whispers to Henri. "I just needed to... I need to help someone. And then this opportunity kind of ... came up. Plus, I honestly don't know any other way a music student can make the kind of money I need this fast."

Henri stays quiet for a long time, then nods. "People make choices. It does not mean anything about who you are."

"I think it does," says Justin. He closes the menu and pushes it to the table's edge. "Anyway, it's not that bad, really. That sexual, I mean. Mostly I just play guitar for her, and she falls asleep in my arms after. She wants to talk, you know? I get that. I feel sorry for her, really. She seems incredibly... lonely."

"Coffee?" Sarah offers.

"God, yes," Justin answers.

"Can I get you anything from the menu?"

"I'll have the blue cheese burger with the Portobello mushroom, please. And... are the fries any good?"

"They're alright," she says, scrunching up her nose. Leaning in close, she lowers her voice to a whisper. "But they're better than the salad, either way. I'm pretty sure it's been in the fridge most of the week."

"Fries it is, then. Thanks." Justin grins.

After Sarah jots down the order, she tilts her head to one side.

"Do I know you?" she asks. "Wait—are you Mary-Beth's little brother?"

The soft lines of Justin's mouth slowly curl into a frown.

"Yeah," he says. "You went to St. Francis?"

"I was in her grade, but we only had English together, I think. We hung out a bit, though. How is she? I heard..."

"Yeah. Well. I guess everyone's heard something."

Sarah takes a step back from the table.

"Sorry," she says. Henri can see the apology in her eyes.

"No." Justin sighs. He runs a hand through his thick hair, tugging at it along the way. "I'm the one who should be sorry. It's not your fault. She's doing badly. And bad things have happened. But I'm not giving up on her yet."

Sarah nods in agreement. Henri can tell that Justin's honesty, and his commitment to his sister, whatever has happened to her, resonate with Sarah's sense of good.

"Where is she?" she asks.

"Etobicoke. She hooked up with this creepy dealer there. It's not a good scene."

Sarah nods again. Henri wonders if Sarah is only expressing sympathy, or if she, too, has seen hardship up close.

"She had a great voice," she says, wistfully. Her smile is quickly reflected on Justin's lips, and Henri can tell that they are, for a moment, both in another place and time.

"Yeah," says Justin. "She did."

"Don't give up on her."

"I won't. Thanks."

As Sarah turns, Justin adds, "Oh! And I don't want to push, but if you could put a rush on the burger, I'd appreciate it. I have to leave pretty soon."

"No worries," she says, glancing around at the field of empty tables. "I'll move you straight to the top of the list." When she winks at Justin, Henri feels a sudden, unexpected heat surge up the back of his neck. It takes him a moment to recognize it as jealousy. He smiles at himself.

"What are you smiling about?" asks Justin.

"Oh, nothing," says Henri. "I was just realizing that I'm still here."

"So, what's your major?" Agnes asked Henri the first time they met. They were in Henri's apartment, but it was his roommate who was throwing the party.

"Urban planning," he told her. He was halfway through his master's thesis, but he didn't volunteer this information, in case his added years, if she hadn't already noticed them, would scare her off. "What year are you in?"

"Third. In art history."

"The history of any type of art in particular, or just all of it in general?"

"I'm narrowing it down."

She tilted her head to one side in mock consternation. She smiled.

Henri felt his chest warm. For the first time, he contemplated the English term "heart-melting." He had never considered it could be a literal thing.

Agnes was shorter than Henri. She looked up at him as she spoke.

"I'm actually a fan of abstract expressionism," she said. "Dali, in particular."

"Ah, The Persistence of Memory."

"Like that."

"I believe in persistence."

"I'll bet you do."

Justin opens the rear door of the Lexus in a gallant sweep and holds it wide for Ms. Winchester. Once she is tucked inside, he comes around the car. Henri holds the opposite door open for him.

"Thanks for picking up the tab," Justin whispers before climbing in. "I never would have made it back otherwise. I'll cover you next week. I promise."

"No need, sir," Henri replies, bowing slightly toward Justin as he clicks the door gently shut.

Everyone from prom teens to porn stars have appreciated Henri's unerring politeness and noble treatment. For Henri, though, his work has had the effect—at times disorienting, at times comforting—of proving again and again that neither a person's morality nor import can be assumed from evidence so misleading as their manners or heel height or the company they keep.

The first drops of rain start to fall as Henri pulls out to return Justin to the coffee shop.

By College Street, the tap-drop-tap on the hood has turned into a steady sluice against the windshield. The wipers lob themselves at the deluge of water, but they make almost no improvement on Henri's view. Stopped in front of the museum,

Henri reaches for one of the spare umbrellas beneath the front passenger seat. Then he imagines Ms. Winchester's husband asking her where she got it.

No evidence, then. Henri looks back at Ms. Winchester.

"Don't bother getting out," she says to him. "It's terrible out there."

"It is my job, after all, Madame."

"That's alright." She opens the door herself, raising her voice to be heard over the crash of the rain. "The least I can do is open my own door."

She thrusts it shut behind her, and with a single step, Ms. Winchester disappears beyond a sheet of water.

Blurred traffic lights shine like tri-colour lighthouses at the end of each block, guiding Henri back to the rented parking spot two blocks from his condo.

"So, have you had a chance to think about it?" Sarah asks as she pours Henri's coffee.

The detective has discovered a second body, hidden beyond a vale of trees. An older man. Stabbed, instead of strangled like the young woman. Both victims have been found half-undressed. Henri's detective suspects an interrupted liaison.

"I have definitely been considering it." Henri notices a small plate crowned with a piece of chocolate pie has appeared next to his coffee. It's his favourite dessert, although the deli is usually out by the time Henri arrives.

"I saved you a piece," she says.

"You, young lady, are trying to woo me." Henri arches an eyebrow.

"I guess I am. Well, not like that, of course." She giggles.

Henri smiles so hard he feels the muscles in his cheeks cramp a second later.

"You make a very good case," he says. "But..."

"But what? What could be better than this? You get to help people. People who really need it. And it doesn't cost us a thing. Other than a tiny bit of gas money. And some time."

Henri looks at Sarah. Her hair frames her face with dark, brown swirls. Her smile is as open and honest as ever. Her eyes are pleading with him to help her. He realizes, too, that she probably thinks her project could help him, as well.

"We'll try it once," he says. "And I'll see if it's practical. Okay? It's all I can commit to right now."

"Okay," she says, her smile broad and open. "That's great. That's all I ask. Come by here at 5:30, okay?"

"I'll be here. Do you need any help boxing up the food?"

"No. It's quiet by then, so I usually have plenty of time to prep everything before close. But thanks."

As Sarah turns to walk away, Henri reaches out and touches her lightly on the wrist to slow her.

"Sarah?"

"Yes?" She turns back.

He wonders what she might be thinking he will ask.

"That young man," he says.

"From last week?"

"Yes. What do you know about him?"

"Not much, I guess. I went to school with his sister, but he was just a kid then." She tilts her head. For a moment, she is Agnes. "You don't know him that well?"

"No." Henri looks away, focuses on the soft yellow of the streetlamp outside. "It's... complex."

"I doubt that."

Her answer catches Henri by surprise. He looks her in the eye, and his look is a question.

"I find nothing's ever as complicated as people think it is," she says. She smiles at Henri in a way that Henri has not seen her smile before. She heads back to her counter, still grinning. Henri feels as if she has peaked through the years and his pain like they were gossamer. She has glimpsed something deep inside of him. But he's not certain what.

"What would you do if I died?" Agnes once asked. They were lying in bed in their apartment off of Sherbrooke Street. Agnes had just started her PhD at McGill. Once Henri's citizenship had come through, he was able to start his first land development project. It had been a huge success and he was gathering investors for a second multipurpose, environmentally friendly downtown condo.

"Don't ask me such a thing," he said.

Agnes rolled toward him, put her hand on his chest.

"I'm serious," she said. "What would your plan be?"

"I would have no plan. You are my everything," he said. He meant it. The idea of life without her had never occurred to him since she had said yes to his proposal at the Musée des beaux arts three years earlier.

"I would want you to remarry," she said.

"Agnes, my heart, I am serious, too. Please do not talk any more about this. Why would you bring up such a thing?"

"Do you think you would choose a man or a woman, after me?"

"I would not choose anyone. Now stop it. I'm going to sleep."

"Spoilsport."

Henri wrapped his arms around her and pulled her close. He rested his chin on the top of her blonde head. She curled into him, kissed his chest.

"You will never die," he whispered. "I will not let you."

Henri knows it's him when the double doors swing open at 10:35.

"Burger and fries?" he hears Sarah call from the counter.

"Hey, yeah! That would be awesome. Thanks!" Justin's voice, rich and young, is filled with the buoyant notes of surprised gratitude.

"I like her," he tells Henri as he slides into the booth. "She's a great waitress."

"That she is," says Henri. A swell of pride washes over him. He chastises himself for the emotion, telling himself it's not his to feel.

"Your woman is sleeping?" Henri asks. A song lyric. Ridiculous. And mean, he knows.

Justin's reaction is immediate, his jaw jutting up in preparation for a second hit, his eyes suddenly hard. He stops in the middle of sliding his leather jacket off.

"She is not my woman."

"I'm sorry," says Henri, and he is. Henri's not sure for whom, exactly, his sudden flash of anger was meant, but it wasn't for Justin. Henri feels a surge of sorrow like tears. He closes his eyes. He still sometimes, randomly, feels like crying, although the tears are no longer there.

Instead there is silence. Henri takes a deep breath to regain himself. He opens his eyes.

Justin's jacket is off. *His eyes are nearly as blue as his hair is black*, thinks Henri. Justin reaches across the table, places his hand over the back of Henri's.

Henri's thoughts leave him for a moment. For a moment, everything is truly quiet.

They are still looking into one another's eyes when Sarah arrives with Justin's coffee.

Henri's hand flinches. He feels Justin grip very softly to persuade him to keep it in place. To stay focused. Sarah says nothing. She has poured Justin's coffee. She is refilling Henri's mug.

The whole world is Justin's eyes—and Sarah's affection, too, which he can feel emanating from her like warmth.

"Would you like to come with us tonight?" Sarah asks Justin. Her voice is soft and gentle. There is a spell at work, and she does not want to be the one to break it.

"Where are you going?" Justin looks up at her, Henri's hand still beneath his.

As Sarah explains the plan, Justin turns Henri's hand over beneath his without looking. He slides his index finger to rest between the veins of Henri's wrist. It is an unabashedly sexual move. Henri feels his heart actually skip a beat.

"That's really cool," he says, still quietly. "Would you mind if I join the two of you, Henri?"

After two years of thinking, there is suddenly no time left to think more. Henri senses Agnes somewhere, prompting him. *Do this*, she impels him. Or maybe it's his own mind, pushing him forward. *Do this. You're not dead yet.*

"Please do," Henri says. He has not taken his eyes off of Justin.

Justin grins.

"Aren't you afraid she'll wake up sometime without you there and be angry?" asks Henri.

Justin nods to the remains on his plate, offering Henri some of his fries. Henri takes one, although he knows the taste won't follow well on the chocolate pie.

"Not really," says Justin. "I'm almost at my goal, anyway. And she's a surprisingly sound sleeper for someone with that much angst."

For the first time, Henri imagines Justin and Ms. Winchester in the hotel room together. He cannot imagine them having sex, although they must. But he can imagine her pouring her heart out to Justin. What must she tell him is wrong with her life?

"And what is your goal?" he asks Justin.

"To help my sister."

"I remember what you said to Sarah last week, but how can you help someone with such problems?"

Justin stops picking at his food. "Because I love her," he says, shocked.

"No," says Henri, embarrassed that Justin has misunderstood him. "I mean how can you go about it, to try to fix these types of problems? It does not seem like something someone else can do for another person."

"Oh. Sorry. I get sensitive about anything to do with Mary-Beth, I guess."

"That's alright. I wish I had had a brother like you."

Justin looks back into Henri's eyes again. *So easy to fall into*, thinks Henri.

"You're a sweet man," says Justin. "Sweeter than you let on." Justin leans back against the bench. "What happened to you, Henri?"

Henri pauses for a moment. Then he hears himself say "My wife died." With the words already out loud, he keeps going before he can argue with himself or draw himself back inside. "It was just over two years ago. She was pregnant with our little girl, and she had an aneurism in the shower and died, and that's where I found her. After they buried them, I sold my holdings and my corporation in Montreal. I moved here, and I started a car service in a city where I did not know anyone, so that no one would ask me how I was holding up. Because I wasn't. And I was not sure I ever would again. And I did not want to be monitored and checked up on and analyzed and judged for how I felt and how I was keeping Agnes, or letting them go."

The young man is holding Henri's hand across the table. He squeezes tight.

"After you drop Beatrice off tonight, would you pick me up again?" Justin asks, then catches what he has said. "Ms. Winchester, I mean."

Henri takes a long, deep breath, and it feels like the first in a long time. He starts to consider the possible repercussions of saying yes, then stops himself. Agnes in bed, the sound of the Montreal jazz festival in the distance, her voice as she promised, "I would want you to."

"Alright," he answers.

11:36 p.m. Henri holds the door for Ms. Winchester. She gets out of the car, straightens her skirt. Henri noticed as soon as he saw them come out of the hotel that she was not clinging to Justin as usual. They also didn't kiss each other goodbye before he got out at the coffee shop. Henri looks at Ms. Winchester closely for the first time. Her grey skirt suit is expensive, but her raincoat is rumpled. Pale, blue irises pattern the collar of her white blouse. Her face has too many wrinkles for her age. She returns Henri's gaze.

"What must you think of me?" she says.

Henri considers her question.

"I am simply your driver, Madame. It should not matter what I think."

Her expression grows sadder, the lines around her mouth deeper. She looks toward the path she normally takes. Henri has always assumed it leads back to her car, parked carefully just beyond sight. He pictures her driving home, alone.

"If, however, it matters to you to know," says Henri, "I think you are like the rest of us. You are finding your solutions where you can. Whether they are the right solutions for you, only you can know. But another person's search is not something anyone else should have the right to judge."

Henri sees tears rise at the corners of her eyes. With a tight smile, she keeps them from spilling over.

"Thank you," she says quietly. She holds out her hand, and Henri shakes it.

"It has been a pleasure doing business with you," she says.

The comment confirms Henri's guess. He pushes past the urge to grin.

"The same," he says to her, realizing he means it. "Good luck."

She smiles at him, her face lightening for the first time since she left the hotel.

"Thank you," she says. "I think I may need it."

"I doubt that."

"Why?"

"I have a certain idea that perhaps you, too, have needed to be reminded of who you are, and then to go back to being that person, if you can. That is not luck so much as... hope, I suppose."

Henri feels a rush of anger at himself for overstepping with a client.

"They told me you own the company," says Ms. Winchester after a moment.

"They're not supposed to do that."

"So I imagine. Anyway, goodbye, Henri. You've been very kind."

"Goodbye, Ms. Winchester."

Henri can see Justin through the window. He is drinking coffee slowly from a wide-rimmed mug, blowing the foam across the surface before each sip. Henri watches from across the street. There is no question that Justin is beautiful.

The weight of years and hurt press back down on Henri for a moment. *There was a time*, he thinks, *a time when everything didn't feel like this.*

Breathe, he hears Agnes whisper. *Just breathe. It's going to be okay.*

Henri breathes.

"Thank you," Henri whispers to the air around him, to Agnes.

He imagines he hears her say, *I want you to be happy. I need you to be happy.* Her voice sounds close. But rather than immobilizing him with longing for her, it frees him.

"I love you," he whispers softly to the night at the edge of the street.

I know, he hears her answer. Her words are as clear as the hush of traffic rushing by.

Henri pictures the evening ahead. Justin. Sarah. Homeless people who need muffins. A sister who needs salvation and may or may not be able to accept it. A stranded, aging man who needs rescuing from the island he built for himself.

Henri promises himself, promises Agnes, that, somewhere in this evening, he will keep an eye out for hope.

Go, prompts Agnes, and Henri crosses the busy street to the café door.

Sunday Brunch

1968

Clarissa slings her backpack onto the ledge, tugs her jacket off, and slides in next to Ted at their booth. She smiles that smile, leans in close to the gang, says something delightful. They all laugh with her; her hazel eyes are alight in the sunshine. Every week a different friend or friends. Sometimes her brother, his man of the month. Sunday brunch, 11:00 a.m. It's their thing.

1983

Clarissa spreads their bags out on the ledge, unbuttons her coat, takes her spot next to Brian, asks the kids what they want. "Grilled cheese! Extra extras!" shouts their daughter. There comes the eye-roll from the boy, growing too cool for his sister's enthusiasm, but still easily cajoled into humour. Sunday brunch with spills of laughter, crayoned dragons on the placemats, strategies for adventure.

2003

Clarissa sets her purse on the ledge, sits down at her table, fans herself with a folded napkin. Clarissa alone, or with friends, or her daughter when she's in town. Sometimes her brother, his husband. Anyone can tell it hasn't been easy, but she's started coming back every week. They're each doing their best, plying her with jokes until she smiles at least the memory of that smile.

2008

Clarissa slides her cane from sight beneath our table, sits down next to me, takes my arm. Our children say we're ridiculous; our grandkids say it's romantic. Forty years of Sundays. How could we have missed each other for so long? I say I must never have noticed her before. A small stroke a few weeks ago has made it hard for her to smile, but her eyes shine, and that's enough.

Optical Illusion

There is a sign taped high up on the plate glass window, behind the tarnished, brown upright piano, that reads: "Anyone who wants to can play." Of the public, most who try are children who have slipped slightly away, still within view of their parents' hunt for soft avocados, or who have escaped the inching line-up for thinly sliced prosciutto. Management's unwritten rule is a maximum of one hour per player, but Moller is allowed to play from 1 p.m. to 5 p.m. every Saturday because he is good for business. Both Moller and the store manager have noticed that every week more people seem to plan their shopping purposely for when Moller is playing.

The produce staff, their heads nodding in time as Moller's fingers dance the keys to Cole Porter, appreciate that the chaos of their Saturday shift has become tempered by deftly played classic jazz, rather than frenetically punctuated by seven-year-olds practicing "My Bonnie Lies Over the Ocean."

At his best, Moller likes to think of himself as a calming influence on the typically hectic whirl of the downtown neighbourhood. Over the past year, he has felt himself gently being woven into its tapestry. It is something he has never felt before in any place, or with any people, and it is a process he has surprised himself by not entirely resisting. Some of Saturday's parents have asked him if he would consider giving lessons to their children. He was invited to last month's staff Christmas party. Ayumu, an amateur classical pianist with a love for mostly Baroque, used to come nearly every week to watch and listen as Moller played. He calls Moller "maharaja." They both know it's what Duke Ellington used to call Oscar Peterson.

But Ayumu, his passion as thin as his frame, is no Ellington, and Moller, having lived too long without joy, is no Peterson. Either way, Moller has noticed that Ayumu's presence is no longer as consistent as it once was. Moller has heard from a friend in the warehouse that it has been weeks since Ayumu last came to play for his hour on Thursday evenings.

Jullie waves to Moller from the display of imported cheeses. She pivots her cart in his direction, then parks her little cage behind the short tower of the piano, next to a chilled, metal bed stocked with iceberg lettuce and designer dressings. Her broad, white smile sparkles at him. Today's scarf is a sea of burgundy sketches of tiny sailboats bobbing on three shades of translucent yellow. Moller thinks he can hear the miniature bells at the bottoms of her silver, chandelier earrings chiming a singsong over the high notes of "Just a Gigolo."

Moller doesn't think Jullie is interested in him sexually. He thinks it would be rude to ask her orientation, but she has mentioned having at least two ex-girlfriends, including an ex-fiancée. The fact that she is interested in Moller in any way creates a tangle of thoughts and feelings he always tries hard to ignore while playing. Aside from feeling flattered by Jullie's attention, he also feels what he tells himself is a sense of paternal benevolence toward her. Yet, he also finds her, often simultaneously, both naively charming and slightly annoying for her continuous offerings of ideas and suggestions for his repertoire and for reviving what he's sure she sees as his faltered music career.

Jullie asks the old man at the nearest table if she can use his extra chair. The man lifts his attention from his spy novel to give her a sharp nod before returning to his murder and espionage. Jullie drags the chair next the piano, to face Moller as he plays. The move blocks a bedraggled blonde woman pushing an enormous baby carriage, her heavy-liddedness accentuated by the grey shadows pooled beneath her blue eyes. The new mother perks up just long enough to bore a vicious glare into the back of Jullie's tangle of curls, before backing her carriage away and circling the seating area to enter from the far side.

Moller plays Gigolo to the end without looking up.

"That was great. I always—" Jullie begins. Moller loses the rest of her comment in the start of "Swinging on a Star."

"Sorry," he says after finishing. "I get caught up in the music sometimes." A handful of patrons dole out a small patter of applause. The spy-catcher drops a toonie into Moller's jar on his way by.

"That's alright. I totally understand," answers Jullie. "I get that way when I'm working on a grant application."

Jullie is a social worker at an immigrant support centre. Moller was born in Kitchener, Ontario, only five hours to the south, but he sometimes wonders from what strange land Jullie must thinks he has arrived. He pictures sitting in Jullie's office to learn the customs of Canada: This is how we do our taxes. This is how we take our shoes off at the door. This is how we work our entire lives, in the hope of someday having nothing left to do. This is how we have conquered the wilderness. This is how we visit it. This is how our children leave us. This is how we barbecue. This is social security. This is universal health care. This is cat food. This is a nursing home. These are our funerals.

"Would you like to go for coffee afterward, today?" asks Jullie.

Moller's fingers are still resting on the keys, his fingertips humming with the need to play more.

"I still have another hour," he says.

"That's okay. I'll do some shopping and come by when you finish."

She has worked this out, he thinks. He looks at the tip jar. Someone has put in a ten today. He didn't notice who it was, but he hopes, for their sake, they took change.

"Alright," he says. "But this time it's on me. I can't keep taking advantage of my fans like this. It will go to my head."

"No promises," says Jullie. "You deserve payment. I love to hear you play." The corners of her eyes crinkle in a way that reminds Moller of his wife, many years ago.

Jullie comes by the piano, as promised, at exactly 5:00. She is carrying a long, whole wheat baguette and a small, crocheted grocery bag filled with clanking jars and fresh vegetables. Daniel in the back has agreed to keep Moller's things a bit longer today, while Moller has coffee with Amanda at the café across the corner.

Jullie tells Moller about the goings on in her life: her cat, her friends, her family in Cambridge, the books she is reading, and more about her past, her connection to jazz—the albums her father would play for her, the music her tap teacher chose when she was a girl, the competition she won when she was 16.

"I never had any real talent," she says, "but I guess I won on sheer effort."

Moller asks enough questions to keep the conversation going, but not enough, he hopes, to lead her on in any way. He is, as ever, uncertain what she wants from him. He is nearly 50 and knows he looks older; she is no more than 30. She told him her father died when she was a teenager, and this may explain some of their odd relationship. But not, he feels, all of it.

"Fred, can I ask you something?" she says.

"Of course."

"Where did you learn to play so well?"

Jullie hasn't asked Moller many questions about himself before, and those that she has, Moller has deflected with enigmatic truths. His contributions to their conversations have largely taken the form of social or artistic commentary, vague expressions of interest in Jullie's life, and discussions about the styles and lives of famous composers. He had been hoping their conversations would continue to be otherwise largely one-sided.

"Oh, I was trained," he answers, thinking through how much truth he is willing to speak. "A long time ago. In Toronto.

There was a conservatory there that my mother was adamant I should get into. My father wasn't as... enthusiastic. But I went."

"How did you do, if you don't mind my asking? Because I would think you must have done very well." Jullie leans forward as if this will help draw Moller's story out of him.

Moller allows himself to tell Jullie the basics of that time. He lets himself picture the conservatory. His first real concert. An ache of memory builds hot and slow in the centre of his chest. He swallows it down with a deep, warm drink from the black coffee for which Jullie did, finally, let him pay. She insisted, though, on buying him a piece of cake to go with it.

"I did," he continues. "I did very well. And I loved it." For a moment, he is who he says he is.

They are sitting in the soft, leather chairs surrounding the electric fireplace at the back of the café. The ceramic fragments of the mosaic table top between them glint in the last rays of the sunset.

"That's what I figured. But, well, it makes me wonder..."

Moller notices Jullie is growing uncomfortable. Her gaze is fixed on the intricately painted chips of Portuguese tile as she prepares her next question.

Moller's muscles tense with foreboding. He has been a fool. Like everything else that has happened, this conversation, Jullie's friendship, is not at all within his control. Self-indulgent, he thinks. I've ignored where she has been slowly steering this for months. He pictures him driving her out to the plains. No. To Toronto, into the city.

"I'm sorry if I'm asking something that's rude," she continues. Her eyes plead with Moller to tell her it is okay to ask, even if it isn't. "I know I tend to overstep sometimes, so please just tell me if you think I am, but I know I'm not the only one who's been wondering why you play a public piano at a grocery store when it seems you play well enough to cut albums or to be in a band or an orchestra or that sort of thing."

The look on Moller's face is clearly not what she had wished for, so she continues in the hopes of improvement.

"I really don't want to offend you," she says, "but I'd like to think that we're friends, and I'm really curious: Why don't you play professionally? Have you ever?"

"Jullie," Moller answers. His mouth shapes the word awkwardly. With precise care, he sets his coffee mug next to his empty cake plate. "I think if you have not learned it yet, you will likely learn soon enough in your life that things do not always work out the way you might have intended."

Of all the staff at Kleghorn's Independent Grocer, Daniel is the only one who knows where to find the pianist outside of the store. Moller had trusted him never to tell anyone. More than that, Moller trusted him, period. Even now, no one at the store knows it was Daniel who talked Moller into coming to look at the piano that first day, or who went with him to the Salvation Army thrift store to buy him a change of clothes and a decent pair of shoes, so he could come back and play.

Daniel had been the only one—in the store, or anywhere— to recognize Moller. But even Daniel, who knew who Moller had once been, didn't know how Moller came to be where he was now. It was something Moller had refused to discuss.

Daniel was walking home from the bars at closing time late last summer when he saw a homeless man sitting next to Oscar Peterson at the corner of Albert and Elgin. Under the streetlight's orange candescence, the former music professor's bulky, brown winter coat looked nearly as bronze as the shiny monument at which he sat.

The piano bench was designed with room for a partner, but Oscar seemed destined to always play his topsy-turvy piano alone, the city's bureaucrats too timid or too short on art or joy to take a seat next to the affable musician and play his massive piano alongside him.

Daniel, coming closer, thought the brush-bearded man looked vaguely familiar. It was a sense drawn mostly from the man's posture as he silently mimed his playing into the air, rather than anything hinted at by the vagabond's mostly obscured face.

"Hey," called Daniel, full of beer and good will, "nice to see someone actually being friendly to old Oscar."

When the man stopped and looked up, Daniel found himself looking into the eyes of his old piano theory professor.

Daniel had taken the class as part of a musical arts degree that, fourteen years later, had yet to land him a relevant job, save for some occasional work laying tracks for a cartoon company in Montreal. Moller was once well-known in the right social and musical circles as an excellent jazz pianist. The grumpy professor had played in the Toronto Symphony Orchestra, had gone on loan to Boston and Prague, and, according to both rumours and album liners, had helped prop up more than one rising jazz vocalist. Daniel had asked and been told by other students that Professor Moller had decided two years earlier to leave the travel and the arbitrary paycheques of a professional musician's life in favour of consistent time with his family and a stable teaching job. Daniel was thrilled at the prospect of having him as a teacher. But, as the semester wore on, Daniel's excitement steadily abated. Professor Moller and Fredrick Moller the musician seemed to have been two different people. Professor Moller was an introverted, unhappy man, who, it turned out, could explain, but never really teach, music.

"Professor Moller?" Daniel asked, standing on the corner. He was only three feet from the statue and the man, and he had no doubt who it was.

Moller's look was one of terror. His fingers drew back reflexively from the space between him and the curved bronze keyboard. His eyes were jarred wide with the startle of being recognized, the fear of what might come next. He continued to gape soundlessly at Daniel until Daniel considered the man might not actually be able to answer him.

"Professor Moller. What are you doing here?" Daniel stopped himself from adding "like this?"

The former professor, regaining his movement, began to scuttle for his duffle and backpack, which were tucked beneath the piano. Daniel instinctively moved over to block Moller from swinging his legs around the bench to stand up and, Daniel was certain, try to escape. It was unbelievable to Daniel this was the man he had known before; the strangely hollow and always composed man who had said that without passion there is no point in creating art, but without a plan there is no point in having passion.

"Don't tell anyone," Moller finally said. His eyes were still wet with panic, and he sounded as though his vocal chords had been shredded and then elaborately rebuilt out of steel wool. Later, he would tell Daniel that that night had been the first time he had spoken in weeks.

Not far from the same statue, Daniel finds Moller sheltered in the alcove created by one of the many corrugated, concrete corners of the grey and brown National Arts Centre. Moller is sharing the warmth of a large heating grate with an elderly hobo and his dog. Daniel has seen the white-bearded man and his German Shepherd sitting on downtown street corners, cheerfully making small talk and collecting change from the relentless, black-coat throng of young office workers. The dog, a red and white bandana around its neck, is lying directly on the grate, its head calmly resting on the old man's legs. Neither the dog nor the man offer a reaction to Daniel's arrival, leaving any response to Moller alone.

"I don't want to go back," Moller says before Daniel can start with "Hello."

"I gave it a shot," Molller goes on. He is looking past Daniel, along the bridge and past the railings to the canal beyond. "You asked me to give it a shot, and I did." His hands, inside the worn wool of his gloves, play each other in the air above his knees. "It's just too far away from me, Daniel."

Moller is sitting propped against his duffle. Stacked against Moller's backpack, Daniel recognizes a third bag. The black, canvas sack holds Moller's dress shoes and the rest of his Saturday kit. By the time Moller stopped playing three weeks ago, his wardrobe had expanded to at least three different dress shirts and two pairs of good pants. The week before, Daniel had helped him pick out a pair of reading glasses. Moller's tip jar had been filling up faster every week. He had started to buy sheet music.

"Would it help if I told you that people have been asking after you? A lot of people? Customers. Staff. Even Kleghorn himself heard you weren't coming anymore. He called the manager. He wants to put you on salary, if you'll come back."

Moller continues to watch something out beyond the traffic of taxis and buses and the occasional smart car.

"No," he says after another moment. "It wouldn't help. Although, you can tell him I appreciate the offer. And you can tell the others they were a good audience. If you like." His hands keep moving—small, insignificant motions that never stop. Daniel wonders, not for the first time, how much control Moller has over his actions. In the store, he always pulled it together somehow. It's no surprise that no one ever guessed he was homeless. Out here, though, there is, yet again, a different Moller.

Three weeks of growth have already grizzled Moller's face into a muted grey haze. The warm air rising from the grate is making it obvious that Moller has no longer been showering. In the final weeks of his tenure at the store, Moller told Daniel he had been saving his tip money each week so he could afford a shared room at the hostel on Friday nights, could shower and eat like an individual instead of part of the mass of homeless at the shelter.

"At least tell me what happened. You were doing so..." Daniel hesitates to say "so well;" he doesn't want Moller to feel like Daniel is patronizing him. Daniel had never meant for the man to be his project. He had had respect for him, both as a largely disliked professor and as a person, the night he found him next to Oscar. But he became caught up in the success of returning a seeming lost man to the folds of society.

Moller is looking away, in the direction of Oscar, who is hiding beyond the Centre's next corner. Moller clears his throat roughly, spits into the grate.

"I wasn't doing well, Daniel," he says, shaking his head in agreement with himself. "I was getting worse every day that I looked like I was getting better."

Daniel sees tears at the creases of his former professor's eyes.

"I've been out of doors for nine years. But where I was before was even worse than that, in so many ways. I'm not what you think I am, Daniel. It has been kind of you, but the man you remembered wasn't even that man back then. He was an illusion. I suffered every day trying to be what other people wanted me to be. I let life's decisions happen to me until I blamed everyone around me for my situation. I had so much hate. But out here, I don't have to hate anyone. I don't have to be anything at all. I can just let it go."

Professor Moller closes his eyes, draws the warm, food-stained air in deeply, then releases it, calmer. His hands have stopped, for the moment. Daniel does not know how to respond. Moller sighs again, less deeply, straightens himself.

"You offered to let me have it back," Moller continues. He is looking at Daniel now, his expression peaceful, earnest. "And it was tempting. It was. But which part of it would I get back? The part where I had dreams? Where I think I can become world-famous? Or even acknowledged? Make my own records? Make enough money to survive by doing what I love? Or the part where I fall in love with the most gorgeous girl I ever met, support a family, buy a house with a garden like the one my mother had, learn to barbecue like my uncle, afford dinner out with my wife? Which one would I choose again now? Which one would I grow to resent more every day until I can't see my wife for the bills, can't see my children for the time I could have been playing and will never get back? Can't see the music for the great stretches where it takes me away from the ones I love?"

"Is that what happened to you?" asks Daniel. Still standing out on the sidewalk, off the grate, Daniel feels his legs getting colder, the strong breeze blowing steadily through the denim of his jeans. He chides himself for complaining, even inwardly, when the two men in front of him spend each day in the cold with no warm apartment to return to afterward.

"Nothing happened to me, Daniel. I happened to me," says Moller. "You and Jullie, you've both just been trying to help me. And you have. I played again. And that was wonderful. So I thank you. But then Jullie—she looks so much like my eldest girl—she wanted to know more about me. I was telling her about how things were for me before I met my wife. Before the girls and the rest of life happened, before I tried to renege on my dedication to all the things I had started out wanting. And I was thinking 'Life just happens to you, Fred. Over and over, life just keeps happening to you. And here it is, happening again, taking away another choice, another opportunity.' But life doesn't just happen to anyone. It never just happened to me. I was lost out there in society, making stupid decisions. But they were my decisions. And in the end, it was never my decisions that brought me down; it was the making of them. I couldn't handle having to choose."

Moller's fingers have started to stir and gnash in short reaches against the air again.

"Speaking with Jullie," he says, "I could suddenly see what would have happened if I had made different decisions. It would have ended the same way. I would have been travelling from city to city, maybe making it a bit further, maybe not, maybe a bit of fame here, or another album there. And I would have grown angrier and angrier at the world for not giving me a wife, and a family, and a red brick house like the one I always dreamed I'd live in. I would have resented not having a pension or time to read or anyone to talk with about the little notes that make up the music of the day."

Daniel jerks back slightly in surprise as Moller suddenly bangs a hand against his own chest for emphasis. "It was always *me*, Daniel," he says. He is growing louder, more emphatic. "It was the making of the choices that killed me, that made me ruin it all. And that... that comes from me. That was never anyone else's fault. I could only see what I had in the context of what I didn't."

His lecture has drained the last of the colour from Moller's face, and he crumples back into himself like refuse between the grate and his duffle.

"So if you see that, then accept it now," Daniel bursts. It is too much for Daniel to think the man cannot, will not, change.

"I do," answers Moller, looking back up to Daniel. His eyes have grown grey in the washed out afternoon. "Rick and Mugs and I are heading west. I always wanted to see the coast."

The colourful hobo gives Daniel a brief nod confirming what Moller has said.

"You're staying on the street?" asks Daniel. "That's not a choice." His sudden anger burns away the cold.

"Yes it is," answers Moller. "And it's the only one I want to make anymore."

Daniel tells his manager he tried to visit Moller's apartment, but Moller had left a message with his landlord explaining he had moved out west.

"So, he had been living on the street for years?" Jullie asks a second time. "I thought he might not have been doing so well. But I never would have guessed he was actually homeless."

"You can't tell anyone," says Daniel. "I promised him I wouldn't tell anyone, but I thought it was cruel not to let you know what really happened. I know you cared about him. He said you reminded him of one of his daughters."

Jullie drops back against the soft, leather chair. "I just liked him, you know? He seemed so sad—like he needed to talk. But he never did. The most he ever told me about himself was that last day. I feel like it's all my fault for having pried."

Daniel takes a drink from the white bowl of coffee between his hands.

"Don't think that," he says. "First of all, someone was bound to. He was a trained professional playing cheesy jazz stupidly well in a grocery store food court."

Jullie is studying the patterns in the low tabletop, her red curls spilling across her face. Daniel wants her to believe him.

"But secondly, I think he was going to make that choice no matter what. As soon as the possibility of living a different life became a realistic option. As soon as he had to make a choice, he was going to choose not to."

Jullie nods quietly. The curls bob up and down. Daniel has never spoken to her before. He has only seen her talking to Moller at the store and once across the room at a bisexual drop-in group at the library. The two dozen or so people had mostly talked about restaurants and celebrities. Daniel noticed Jullie had looked as bored as he felt.

Leaving the stock room at the end of his shift today, he spotted her in the condiments aisle and introduced himself as a friend of Moller.

"I didn't know he had any others," she had said, taken aback. "I'm glad." Her smile was broad and bright.

"I'm glad you talked with him," she says, meeting Daniel's eye again. Her own eyes are green and sparkle in the dying light.

"I'm sorry," says Daniel.

"Don't be," she answers, regaining herself. "I guess that's what you get for trying to fix a perfectly good wreck."

"Well, we can always try again with another one. I hear there are a lot of us wrecks out there."

"You've noticed that, too?"

"I have. I can even prove I'm one of them. Would you like to come back to my place and see my fine arts degree?"

Jullie smiles.

"Depends," she says. "What kind of art do you make?"

Anita Dolman

Diana

Poor girl, just a slipshadow. They found her body last week in her apartment, badly beaten. The boyfriend did it. There was no doubt. They found him with her, a bloody bottle still in his hand. You know he was living there for free. I don't care what people say; "retard" or not, she deserved better. Me, I believe we all do. I only talked to her a couple of times. Nice kid. Never would have guessed she was 34. Course, I wouldn't have guessed she was a girl, either, 'til she got to talking.

And talk—boy, could she talk. Talk you up a storm, talk your ear off. Told me all about her family and her job shovelling snow off the canal that winter. Nice kid. I met her sister once. Well, not *met* so much. Guess Diana got all the talking genes in that family. Me and my husband, we didn't see her much before it happened. Everyone knew she'd got in with a bad crowd, though. Oh, the leather jacket, the smoking, and her always tagging after those thugs. You could tell something bad would come of it.

Anita Dolman

Happy Enough

The faded screen door of Kitchisippi Convenience is warped near the handle. The screen separates a little more each week from the faded green wood at one corner. Jeff pulls the door open with a tug to keep it from sticking in the frame. One day, when he has time, he plans to come by with his toolbox and offer to fix it for the old man. Right now, though, it is Monday morning, and Jeff heads for the cookie aisle.

One pack of Chunks Ahoy! cookies every Monday, and an extra-spicy beef stick on Fridays. These are Jeff's secrets from Janine and her regimen of tofu-ham sandwiches on multigrain bread, with their extra lettuce and organic alfalfa sprouts, and a thin spread of fat-free, egg-free, lactose-free sesame-paste mayonnaise, which she packs for his lunch. He tries to take it as an expression of love. But, it's a form of love that's far from easy to accept every day.

"You happy today?" asks Nick, sliding Jeff's change across the plastic lotto display case.

"Happy enough," says Jeff.

"That's good, that's good," says Nick. "You know, you got to stay happy."

On Sunday evening, Janine sends Jeff out to get skim milk for the new fat-free homemade yogurt recipe she's found as a special treat for the kids. The store is surprisingly full, mostly with families choosing their evening movie rentals. Jeff navigates past a brunette holding her toddler to hover over the open ice cream freezer.

"Brown or white, Jimmy? You decide. What will it be?"

In front of Jeff at the counter, two teenaged boys are picking out candy from the open bin next to the cash. Gummy drops shaped like cola bottles and pink running shoes. Is sixteen too old to be buying candied running shoes? Jeff can't remember at what age he would have stopped doing things like that in favor of smoking weed behind the arena, or spending his evenings in Cindy Hanson's rec room. And most kids seem to grow up even more quickly now. Jeff's own kids are three and nine. Still young enough to be dazzled by candy. Not that they're allowed to be.

A deep horn is bellowing its way up the street, the sound building as it gets closer, until the droning fills the store, drowning out the boys' snickers. Nick goes to the window. A black, extended-cab pick-up pulls to a stop out front, parking at a wild angle to the steps. The driver gets out, but the horn continues to bleat its suffocating noise. Jeff's mind goes quickly to every zombie movie he's ever seen.

"Maxwell!" Nick calls out as the door swings open. A middle-aged man with a handlebar mustache grins at the old Italian.

"Hey, Nick!"

The two boys in front of Jeff have already paid for their sugar fix and are heading out the door. The horn stops for a minute, then starts again. Jeff drifts out of his spot in line as if he's suddenly remembered he was supposed to get a movie. Maxwell puts two giant chip bags and a lighter on the counter.

"I guess you heard we won, eh?" he says to Nick. He tips his head toward the truck for a moment, raises his eyebrows in a What-can-I-do? apology.

"Ah, baseball!" Nick exclaims. "It was a big game, then?"

"You haven't been following the Olympics, Nick?"

"Oh, no. No, no, no," he sings, smiling more broadly still. "No time, no time." His hands flutter out like abruptly busy birds, then swoop down to rest on his belly, satisfied at their quick flight.

"My boy's twenty now," says Maxwell. "Got me to go with him to the hotel to watch. Then talked me into driving all over town afterward with the horn going. I tell you, I can't believe I'm old enough to have a twenty-year-old son. It doesn't feel so long ago that I was him."

"Ha. Is not so bad," says Nick. "Wait until you have grandpoppets. Then you feel old, you believe me."

"How are the girls doing? And little Sam?"

"Oh, they're wonderful. Bright as ever. We don't see them enough, of course. My wife would like to see them much more. Especially our little Contessa. She just graduated last year, you know!"

Jeff has never seen "Maxwell" before, had fancied until now that he was one of the only people in town who came into the quiet corner store and talked to Nick in a personal way; maybe the only one to know Nick's name, or about his wife's cancer. Jeff feels a small knot of jealousy, hearing Nick tell someone else about his grandchildren. Jeff never knew he had any. How many does he have? Where would they be? The old country? And where would that be? Sicily? Italy? Which part? How could he have never asked?

The new man reaches into his blue, plaid lumberjack coat and pulls out his wallet.

"My oldest girl, Lori, is fifteen now. And Tina's thirteen. You'd think they'd be more trouble than that one at this stage," he says with a nod back to the truck. The horn has finally stopped. But then it starts again, in short blasts this time, building up to another good, long honk.

The man pays, and Jeff walks his milk back to the counter. He almost picked up a movie for the kids, but Janine is adamant that a three-year-old should be in bed by 7:15 and a nine-year old by 8:00 "no matter what." She's right, of course; structure is good. It's important for kids. Lets them know where they stand. Jeff glances at the comedy section. If they didn't both have so much work to do after the kids go to bed, he and Janine could watch something together, like they used to.

The horn fades away.

Jeff puts the milk on the counter.

"Ah. Mister Jeff. So, you happy today?" asks Nick.

For days, Jeff cannot stop thinking about the man with the mustache. Maxwell is connected enough to life in town that he knows all about Nick's grandchildren, yet Jeff has never met or even seen him before. He's not on the community fair organizing committee or the arts and agriculture board or a member of the NDP. He's never come into Jeff's legal practice or had any dealings involving Jeff, even though Jeff is one of only two lawyers in town.

The man also hasn't been in the town newspaper, which Janine edits, or signed up for the organic food distribution service they and all of their friends are part of. Jeff doesn't even remember ever seeing him shopping or at town council. Or at the rallies to protest the highway expansion. And he would certainly have spotted him if he had ever come to the annual skate-a-thon or the berry festival or the Adopt-A-Ditch.

Jeff asks around. Not a single person he knows knows this guy, or his kids, or his wife, if he has one—at least not based on Jeff's description. Jeff and Janine have lived in Kitchisippi Springs for five years. It would be hard for two people to be more involved in their community than us, thinks Jeff.

Still, neither of them has ever seen or heard of this guy before. Not that they know everyone in Kitchisippi personally, but this guy—this guy would get noticed in a crowd.

Next Sunday, Jeff takes a chance and heads to the store again at exactly 6:00 p.m. Rounding the corner, he catches sight of Maxwell pulling himself up into the cab of his enormous truck. The truck pulls away and heads to the west. Jeff goes into the store all the same. He buys a can of soup too high in sodium for Janine to allow him to eat. He'll have to hide it in the car and take it to work tomorrow.

Nick is still chuckling as Jeff sets the can down on the lotto display.

"That guy," says Nick. "That guy. He is a funny guy."

Jeff can feel his ears perking up like a dog's.

"Oh? How so?" he asks as casually as he can manage—a technique that involves pretending he has misplaced something in his pockets. He and Nick are both looking out the window. The truck is long gone.

"Och, just always with the jokes, you know? Me, I am a terrible one at jokes. No memory. But I like a good joke. You've got to keep happy, you know. You happy today, Mister Jeff?"

"Oh. Yeah. Sure. Happy enough," he answers, slow to remember his line.

"That's good, that's good. Maybe someday I ask you, you say 'Oh yes, Nick. So, so happy,' eh?" Nick rings the can through. "Dollar eighty-five."

"Okay. Say, Nick? Who was that guy anyway, the funny guy in the truck? I don't know him." Jeff digs a handful of coins out of his pocket.

"You don't know Maxwell? Hah. That surprise me, Mister Jeff. Your wife, she edit paper, and you the big lawyer, and you don't know him?"

"No, should I?"

"Well, it is good joke if you do not. You sure no one tell you?"

Jeff shakes his head as he counts out exact change in the palm of his hand. Suspicion is glowing like an ember in the back of his brain, burning slowly down the wick of his muscles. He doesn't like to be the last person to know anything, and he has a feeling he is not about to like what everyone but him knows about Maxwell.

"He was town lawyer, and his wife she edit the paper. They move away with their poppets, oh six, maybe seven, year ago. Come to think, they were a lot like you and your wife. You know, in how they live, what they like. *Involved.* You know."

This is not what Jeff had been expecting. Although he's not sure what he had been expecting. The rough and carefree joker in the flannel jacket, driving a mammoth pick-up through town, was the town lawyer before Jeff? Was married to the newspaper editor? Was "involved?" Jeff's mind grasps at questions to ask, but he only manages to catch one.

"Why is he back?"

"That I do not know, Mister Jeff. It is still a dollar eighty-five, though," Nick says, his open palm hovering over the counter.

Jeff has been holding the coins in his hand throughout their conversation, but had stopped short of putting them either on the counter or into Nick's hand. He quickly sets the money down, stuffs the rest of his change back into his pocket, and heads for the door.

"Thanks, Nick."

"Your soup!" Nick calls.

Jeff stops a foot from the door, turns and stalks sheepishly back to the counter.

"It is really funny you never find out before," says Nick as Jeff scoops up the can.

Jeff is full up to his eyebrows with a feeling he doesn't usually feel, and it takes him most of the walk home to finally identify it as anger. He tells Janine about his discovery as soon as he gets in. She's bathing their little girl. Janine looks up at Jeff from her perch at the edge of the tub.

"Isn't that totally... .weird?" he says. He sounds like an awestruck teenager, and he knows it.

"Huh," says Janine, turning away to put an overboard mermaid toy back in the tub. "She must be Candice Halliwell, then—the editor two editors before me. I've seen her issues. She was alright."

Jeff opens his mouth to say something more. He tries again. An empty feeling pushes at his heart as he watches her back, seals any more words inside of him. Janine laughs at their daughter spraying her own toes with an arc of water from the mermaid's mouth. Jeff listens to their murmuring and splashing as he heads back downstairs to read over a land lease agreement.

Jeff went into business with his friend Leon, who had moved to Kitchisippi ahead of Jeff and Janine. Leon soon found the town too small and boring. He left his half of their small law firm to Jeff within a year of Jeff's arrival.

Jeff calls Leon in Toronto. Leon tells him he first thought of opening shop in Kitchisippi after word spread that one of the two local lawyers was packing up. Leon took on some of Maxwell Olson's case load. He had worked through most of the ongoing cases and business by the time Jeff joined him eight months later. The name Olson does ring a bell with Jeff. Jeff goes through the files at work and sees that Olson appears as the original barrister on some of Jeff's clients' wills and estate records.

Armed now with Maxwell and Candice's full names, Jeff asks Terry, the butcher, about them. Terry is in his sixties and is one of the few people Jeff knows who was actually born in Kitchisippi. He says he knows nearly everyone and everything that has ever happened in town, and Jeff believes him. He is what Janine calls a "historical resource."

"Oh, yeah. That's funny, eh?" says Terry when Jeff mentions the coincidence of Maxwell and Candice's jobs. "I didn't realize that's who you meant when you asked the first time."

"Come to think of it, they were a lot like you folks," says Terry. His cleaver is dangling by the handle from his fist, which is tucked under his chin in pondering position as he leans on the display cooler. "They had a boy and a girl, too, and later another girl, I think. Real joiners like you, too, if you don't mind my saying. It ain't a bad thing. Need you type of folks, you know? Keeps things going, I suppose."

Jeff isn't sure how to feel about the heavily mixed compliment, so he just moves on with his questions.

"What sort of things did they join—I mean, what kind of activities or whatnot did they take part in?"

"Oh, just about everything lefty, I suppose," says Terry, his gaze drifting to the giant rack of lamb in the glass-fronted freezer by the window. Terry is an amazing resource, thinks Jeff, but he doesn't have much of an attention span.

"They were NDPers," he continues, "and she started that organic food distribution whatsit. They were into all them committees and that—them ones for the fair and the gardens and the arts and ag, and the skating. They used to be at town council all the time, causin' a stir, rantin' about the highway expansion. I think they even started the Adopt-A-Ditch. Now, I tell you, who the hell would want to adopt a freakin' ditch? A puppy, sure. A kid, yeah. Even a garden. But a ditch? That's just the damn stupidest thing I... Jeff?" Terry is still talking as Jeff heads out the door.

When Jeff tells Janine about the life lived before them, she tells him it happens.

"It's a pretty small town," she says, sorting their delivery of organic produce into the refrigerator. "How many ways can there be to be liberal in a prairie town?"

Jeff is starting to feel that, caught up in the business of shopping and folding laundry and running the paper and saving the planet and saving the town and gardening and politics and more cooking, Janine has little sympathy left for him. Or for herself, for that matter.

Janine had a wildness and a grace when Jeff met her in university. She wore long, flowing skirts that led people to call her a hippie. She would consume books like meals, talk about changing the world, smile almost constantly, welcome anyone to dinner, tell stories that made Jeff squeak with laughter.

He wonders when the last time was that he saw her sit down to do anything other than work or eat or help the kids with something. He reaches out and places his palm on her back as she pulls corn cobs from the box on the counter. She stops. She stays still for a moment before turning to face him.

"What is it?" she asks.

But the words aren't there, again. He holds her gaze for as long as she'll let him. Then she looks down at her hands, flustered, turns back to the box on the counter.

"I've got to finish this," she says.

Jeff withdraws and heads to his den.

Jeff is trying to process what he feels about repeating someone else's life. He skips the week's town council meeting, forgets to fill out the order sheet for their organic groceries. He infuriates Janine by openly putting salt on his dinner. At the table. In front of the kids.

Jeff goes to the store for milk on Sunday evening. He doesn't leave the house until 5:55, then walks there slowly. There is no truck in front of the store, but something feels out of place as he opens the screen door.

The shiny, new silver handle still under his palm, Jeff stops midway across the threshold. A wave of guilt washes over him as he inspects the new screen, cinched tightly into the grooves of the door. The warp has been sanded down, the door repainted a bright green. It swings smoothly on the freshly oiled hinges as Jeff crosses the threshold the rest of the way .

"Is good work, eh?" asks Nick from behind the counter. "Maxwell, he come and fix it, says it is travesty I still have same, broken door six years later. Me, I never notice so much, but he fix nice, eh?"

Jeff stares at Nick for a moment. He nods his agreement, reopens the door and walks out without a word. Jeff turns in the opposite direction from his house.

The eerie feeling that he is replaceable has nagged at Jeff since he first heard about Maxwell and Candace and their life before his and Janine's. Janine is, as usual, right; being left-leaning in a small town can offer a very limited range of social and political possibilities. But this is ridiculous. And now Maxwell is back. What does he want? Is he planning to start another law firm again? To push Jeff's practice out of town? Reclaim his old clients? Replace Jeff on his committees— or, at least, join him? Would they get along? Vote the same? Argue bitterly?

It is clear the man has dibs on everything, but a person can't just leave and then pick up years later right where he left off. There are consequences. There are people in between. This is Jeff's life now. Even if someone else has lived it before. It is his. His and Janine's.

A terrible thought comes to Jeff. What if Maxwell is divorced? What if he wants to come back to his life *exactly* as it was? What if he wants to marry the newspaper editor? What if he wants Janine?

No, that's just stupid, thinks Jeff. *Now I'm being paranoid. Still, you can't blame me. What are you supposed to think when you find you've accidentally been living someone else's life for five years?*

Jeff thinks of the hundreds of small and significant decisions he must have made over the course of his life to bring him to a single, exact point. What are the odds the inventory of choices in a completely different person's life would lead to the same precise result?

Jeff feels lightheaded. He has fumed and stewed and brooded himself all the way to the ballpark. There is a game at the diamond where Jeff's son plays little league every Saturday. This evening, the field and dugouts are filled with energetic guys in their late teens and early 20s, some with their parents in the stands, some with their girlfriends, some with their own families already, cheering them on from the bleachers. A row of baby carriages and strollers has formed near the fence like an advancing, pastel artillery on the front lines of a children's battle.

Jeff spots the blue plaid of Maxwell's coat in the crowd.

Coasting on a mix of feelings with which he isn't very familiar, Jeff walks to the stands without a plan. He will confront Maxwell. That's what he will do. He will tell him there is a new sheriff in town. He will... do something.

Jeff climbs the bleachers to the fourth row, excuses himself tersely as he passes in front of a plump brunette he recognizes as the woman who runs the weight loss centre. A curl of relish garnishes the corner of her mouth. Two hotdogs wrapped in white paper stick out from the open purse stashed by her feet.

Jeff shuffles further past a teenage girl. She is leaning deep into a vampire novel. On its cover, a complex constellation of pale, mooning stars are backdropped against a foreboding-looking night. An embossed drop of blood oozes down the centre of the image. The girl straightens up to let Jeff pass, her eyes never leaving the pages. She sinks back into her spot on the bleachers.

Jeff passes Maxwell wordlessly and takes the empty spot on his far side.

Jeff stares out at the game for a moment, building courage. Maxwell is cheering on his son, who is pitching.

"Woohoo!" bursts Maxwell. "That's it, Robbie! Keep 'em low!"

Jeff clears his throat, sounding like a toad. Maxwell does not look over, keeps his eyes on the field and his son.

"Hey, you used to be a lawyer, didn't you?" Jeff tries casually, but a fly ball upstages his "Hey" and the cheer of the crowd muffles the rest of his sentence. With the crowd settling again, Jeff rallies his best court voice to recover with a louder "You're Maxwell Olson, aren't you?"

Maxwell turns as if noticing for the first time someone is sitting beside him. Jeff's heart is racing so fast it feels like Maxwell is a high school crush.

"Yep," Maxwell says with a smile. He sticks his hand out to shake.

Jeff takes it and says, "I'm Jeff Barrows. I'm the new lawyer in town." Then he corrects himself. "Well, not that new. Five years now. I heard you were the town lawyer before Leon and I came."

"Good stuff! And I was. How you finding it?" Maxwell's cheerfulness throws Jeff from his trajectory. He had been steaming himself up for a battle. He tries to stay firm and tough.

"Very good. Excellent. It's a good town. My wife and I really like it here." He can't stop himself. He keeps going, laying it all out in case Maxwell isn't actually aware yet of what is going on. "My wife's the editor of the newspaper. Between the two of us, we've gotten really involved in the community. Committees, events, organizing, that sort of thing. Us and the kids."

He can feel the words "So, what brings you back to Kitchisippi?" about to leap from his tongue, but he catches them for fear they'll sound ridiculous. There is only one reason to point out the fact that you have way too much in common with a guy who has been away from town for six years, and it's paranoia. Jeff feels suddenly ridiculous. It's obvious that this is all a bizarre coincidence.

"Oh, yeah?" says Maxwell. The curious tilt of his head and the mild surprise in his eyes shows Jeff that Maxwell must not have known he had been so thoroughly replaced in town.

"Well." Maxwell is deciding something. Then he shakes his head as if what he has decided is that Jeff must be crazy. With a thoughtful nod he adds, "Well, good luck with that."

Jeff is confused. Does he mean good luck replacing him? It's the end of the seventh inning. A number of people in the bleachers below are packing up or heading off to get something from their car, or to change seats to talk with other friends.

"What do you mean?" Jeff asks.

Maxwell looks to the field, but his son is in the dugout now.

"Well," says Maxwell slowly, "I just mean that this is positively a great town. But, I'd be careful about getting too caught up in it."

He turns to Jeff, looks him in the eye.

"Look, I shouldn't be giving you advice," he adds. "The way it went for me... it doesn't mean it'll go that way for you, too. You're a totally different person, and I don't know you from Adam."

Jeff has the tumbling sensation he's about to be told he has made some kind of horrible mistake, like running over a child's dog or accidentally telling his best friend's wife about her husband's mistress.

"No. Please," says Jeff. "Go ahead. What happened with you?"

"Well, my wife, Candice, and I first came to town, oh, over a decade and a half ago now, with our boy. I started my law practice. I thought I could make a real difference here—bring my shiny, new law degree and set up shop to help solve the citizenry's problems, teach them the best and most modern ways to cope with the big, real world. Candice felt the same, I think. She took a job as a reporter at the paper, and in a couple of years she was editor. Then we had a girl, and then a second. We bought a dog. And I guess, step by step, we just got more and more... involved. We started an organic food co-op in town, and it sort of snowballed from there. Next thing I know, we're rallying and organizing and protesting and we've either joined or started almost every community group in town left of the Young Conservatives."

Maxwell looks over to his daughter, who is still deep inside the world of teenage vampire drama. A corner of his mouth edges up into a wistful smile.

Still looking at her, he says "We kept going and going and going until we were running our home like a childrearing and social causes business."

Maxwell brings his attention back to Jeff.

"One day it dawned on me that all of the 'us' had gone out of us. You know?"

Jeff knows. He feels as if Maxwell has jerked a stopper out of his heart—one he had known for a long time was there, but he hadn't been able to exactly name or to find. His body is warming in the cool evening air. His head still feels adrift, but differently so. To ground himself, he focuses on the bobbing, plaid points of Maxwell's collar.

"We had done everything we could to make our kids better, our community better," Max continues, "until we were barely talking to each other about anything that didn't involve diapers or school trips or local politics or planning the next berry festival or something-a-thon."

"So, what did you do?" Jeff asks, his voice coming out so quietly he's not sure Maxwell will hear him.

"I quit!" Maxwell says with a definitive nod.

"Quit what?"

"Well, everything," Maxwell laughs. "Quit the practice. Quit my marriage. Quit town."

Jeff can feel himself openly staring at Maxwell. Someone has just made it home, and the crowd is yipping and clapping. He realizes his mouth is hanging open. He closes it.

"Look," says Maxwell, leaning toward Jeff. His expression is serious under his dark brow. "There comes a point when you realize you've lost what you came for in the first place. I've thought a lot about it," he says. "And I think it's a thing, especially with people with specialized knowledge. Take us. We're lawyers. Take our wives. Editors. Professionally, we all tell people what to do all the time. There comes a point where you think you know everything better, so you join every committee, direct every event, control every little thing that your kids, and then your neighbors, and then complete strangers, are doing. Came a day I woke up and realized I didn't know shit. Who am I to tell people how to live? So I quit. Quit everything. Left to figure out who I'd be if I wasn't just the guy directing traffic."

Jeff is with him on this, has felt the unfurling momentum of the story. But, the idea of leaving everything completely—especially of leaving Janine—unnerves him. He has never even considered it, not once in all their quiet arguments, not even when she told him what to wear or to eat or to say to company.

"What about your wife," Jeff asks. "And your kids?"

Maxwell looks down at his hands. Jeff realizes Maxwell has

been twisting the ghost of a long-gone ring around his left ring finger while telling his story.

"I lost my wife long before I left here," Maxwell says. "She wasn't the same person I'd married. When I told her what I wanted to do, she said she had already become who she was going to be. She said I could go find myself where the hell ever I wanted, but she knew who she was."

Maxwell looks down at his hands, then out to the field again where the eighth inning is well underway.

"She's the publisher up in Creeberg now," he adds. "She tells me she's happy enough. Guess I'll have to take her word for it."

Jeff takes the longest way home possible, walking almost a full circle around the town. The person Max ultimately found when he went looking for himself turned out to be a writer. Max's wife had said he'd be a lousy writer. Max has sold four westerns so far and is working on what he calls "a literary novel." One of the four books he's published has been optioned to become a film. To celebrate, Max has rented a cabin outside of town with his kids for the summer. They wanted to come back and see some old friends.

Jeff and Max have made plans to go for a beer on Tuesday. Jeff said he has a lot of thinking to do right now, but Max has advised him not to take it all so personally.

"In the end, people are their own people," he said.

Jeff does not feel like his own person. Jeff realizes he has not felt like his own person in a long time.

Jeff gets home at midnight. Janine is waiting in front of the TV.

Well, at least she's waiting, he thinks.

He can tell from the silence of the house, though, that she is furious he didn't call. She pretends to be too deeply engrossed in an infomercial for ultra-absorbent socks to notice him when he comes in. He takes his shoes and coat off in silence. She's in jeans and a fair-trade sweatshirt. He watches her profile in the glow from the screen as he comes into the living room. He stops in the archway.

"Babe," he starts. It's what they used to call each other. But now he can't remember the last time he called her anything at all to her face.

Janine turns the TV off with a click of the remote clutched in her hand. Jeff hears Max's wife's words in his head. He tries not to imagine Janine saying the same.

"I got you something," he says. "I've been walking and thinking. I thought I had some thinking to do. And I did. Anyway, I saw that Nick was up late."

Jeff fishes into the plastic grocery bag for his purchase.

"So I got him to let me in."

Janine finally looks toward Jeff, takes him in from head to socks, then back up again. She's taken her contact lenses out already. She has her new, black, rectangular glasses on. She had granny glasses when Jeff met her, but he actually kind of likes these ones, too. They look cute on her, suit her face well. She's still so pretty when she's not angry.

"I don't know if you still like these. I know they're not organic." He approaches her with the cookies held out gingerly, as if approaching a lioness with a steak. "But I know they used to be your absolute favorite, and I thought that... maybe..."

By the time the cookies reach her, Jeff sees the thin stream of tears on Janine's cheek. But what she is looking at is Jeff. She looks at him for a long time. Jeff can't gage her expression or tell what she might be thinking. Normally, he can guess right away. And when he can't, she usually tells him before he can ask. But not right now. Right now, they are each holding onto one end of a cookie bag.

With a deep, sniffling sigh, Janine lets go of her end and pushes the bag gently back toward Jeff. Still looking at him, she removes a box of tissues from the top of their faux-leather ottoman and sets it on the floor. She slides to her knees and lifts the giant lid.

They've owned it for over a year, and Jeff never realized it was that kind of ottoman. Janine pulls an empty bag of Chunks Ahoy! from the box and holds it up to Jeff's full one. Jeff stares in silence for a minute. First at the empty bag. Then at his wife. Then into the ottoman. Aside from several empty cookie bags, Jeff can see the dark box holds a stack of old photo albums, a pair of tinted granny glasses, Jeff's old Cannon AE1 camera, flyers for the photography exhibit he was in in university, several journals he doesn't recognize, and a copy of *1001 Places to See Before You Die.*

Jeff looks back to Janine again. She's still kneeling, looking up at him, the evidence of her secret sublife in front of her. She's smiling at Jeff. It's a wicked smile. She hasn't smiled at him like that in a lifetime. Jeff smiles back.

Anita Dolman

Bureau

Spider at the desk. Never mind, just work and work, and spider crawls, and then the phone and you are, where was he, did he go, I wish you could have seen, yes, I got the email, just a sec, the fax machine is ringing, I hope it's, oh my god, I forgot the file, I have to, I heard you eat three in your life, asleep I mean, I wish I knew, wait, I found, there's the door, I have a meeting, would you mind if we, why don't you, there he is again, my god he's huge, I told you, no we wanted to but, why, I can't, why are you asking me now, you know I have a, please not, then why, you told me that but I still don't, where the hell did he go again so fast, you leave me out of that, you know I don't want, I have to get the door, you just don't understand that, no I have to, I have, I have to go, they're waiting, don't be like that, it's not my fault, you left me, you saw it coming, there he is again, no, I'm not alone, we have to, well, it doesn't work like, it never has, I have to go now. What were you expecting?

Bottle Rockets

Everyone in Group says they're fine this afternoon. Walter, Devon, Gladys, Janet, Kris. But, then, everyone in Group always says they're fine. I've worked at the Centre for five months and not once has a client had a problem they wanted to discuss in Group—except, of course, for complaints about the Centre. One-on-one therapy brings out the real demons of revelation. Group usually plays out like a poker game where all the players are bluffing and everyone has bet it all.

But the therapy is part of the addiction centre's healing plan, so twice a week each counsellor drags their group of clients—the new ones, the old ones, and the ones that just keep on coming back—into the central meeting room in B Wing and seat them in a rough circle of carpeted office chairs, the cardboard seats creaking with every shift of discomfort or boredom.

After trying to talk to Leroy, I fill in his mood today—depressed, introspective, evasive: D, INTRO, EV—on my chart and turn to Gladys, who's beside him. Gladys's current preferred drug is crack cocaine. She's far from the first crack addict I've had, even though our facility is an hour and a half outside of Calgary, and even Calgary is not exactly Los Angeles. Gladys, however, is the first one to have attacked two of her kids with a frying pan, giving one a concussion and breaking the other's arm. But that was over a year ago, and it's not why she's here this time. Not directly.

I know each of my clients got here in their own, complicated way. If a counsellor can't help feeling revulsion toward some of them, if they absolutely cannot stop themselves from judging

171

a client, our training tells us to never show it. Today, Gladys is hiding behind her stringy, shoulder-length black hair. She has made eye contact only with the floor and with my running shoes. I can tell she's worrying about something because she's pinching the material at the knee of her jeans over and over again, tugging it between her thumb and the rest of her fist, even though she's well past her initial physical withdrawal. She's been here for three weeks so far, this time.

"And how are you today, Gladys?" I ask with as much sugar as I can manage.

"Fine," she says flatly, then bites her lip. The truth is no one here wants to hear each other's problems. She's waiting out the rest of her minimum two-month, court-ordered stay. Counting her other stays, I'm her fourth therapist at the Southern Alberta Recovery Centre alone. This time, Social Services has taken the last of her five kids out of her care for good.

"Why don't we pick up where we left off last time?" I ask. "You were going to tell us about your kids."

She was going to do no such thing. It's something she won't talk about, but I'm giving it another shot to see how she'll respond. Last time she said she didn't have any, so I talked about them for her, from her files. The files lacked details, though—no photos, no personal information about what they like, their personalities, so I got creative. The rest of the group picked up the theme, happy with the safe, abstract subject of their kids, their grandkids, their nieces and nephews.

This time, though, Gladys ignores me and continues to stare at a spot on the yellow linoleum a couple of inches in front of my left foot. Her eyes, which few people get to see, are a washed-out green rimmed by black lashes and the typical dark horseshoes of a middle-aged alcoholic-turned-heroine-addict who has given up on the idea of anything that could be described as happiness. Gladys, in fact, immediately distrusts anyone who talks about that sort of touchy-feely bullshit.

Her light-tan complexion is drawn with the deep, sallow wrinkles of lifetime alcoholism, which her file tells me was her starter drug. She looks about 55, and I try not to let her remind me of my mother, although they would have a lot in common. But Gladys is 36—five years older than me.

There have been days at the clinic when I thought I could reach her and get past what the other counsellors haven't been able to. If I could just get her to make direct eye contact with me even once—and keep it.

I've had a small, nagging headache since early this morning and, after a day of meetings and a new patient in A Wing throwing up on me, this doesn't feel like a day for miracles. I hold steady waiting for a response, keep my gaze set on the hair shrouding Gladys's face. Another full minute ticks by on the clock above the door. The other clients' chairs groan against impatient readjustments. I sense the rest of the group watching me watching Gladys, but I stay trained on her. This is one of the tactics I've learned, to show the group I can't be intimidated by silence.

I wonder what Gladys is really thinking about. I try not to get distracted myself, to think about dinner, make a grocery list. I seriously doubt Gladys is thinking of her kids. Her incessant staring at the ground, her greyed sneakers flecked with dirt, the smell of her hair, make me feel a sudden wave of nausea. I look at my watch. I look back at the tangle hiding Gladys's face. She is rubbing both hands slowly over her knees again. I want to grab her by the shoulders. I want to yell at her to snap out of it. I tighten my grip on my pen and keep waiting. The rest of the group keeps fidgeting, watching us both.

Gladys's husband has come to the Centre twice in the past two weeks, pushing past the two gangly orderlies the Centre considers front door security.

The staff isn't supposed to tell Gladys he's been here. It would interfere with her recovery. But it's obvious from her nervousness lately that she knows.

Janet shifts in her chair, then pulls it in a bit to close the circle more tightly. The move scrapes the metal feet across the linoleum, and the screech fills the silence I know I've let go on far too long. Gladys flinches, straightens, and catches sight of Janet, her frizzy red hair in wild curls and her eyes big in surprise and embarrassment at suddenly being the centre of attention. But Gladys only throws a mean look to somewhere around Janet's shoulders and returns her focus to the lino, tugging all the while at her jeans. There's something about her tugging and tugging on the extra denim over her scrawny knees I can't bear to watch any longer. I decide to let it go and not ask Gladys anything else today.

I move onto Walter, a fat drunk in his 50s, the kind who makes the world's rehab centres and AA meetings go 'round— an otherwise nice guy with a bad habit, whose wife's given him his final me-or-the-booze ultimatum and who, after enough sessions, weeks or meetings, will admit, although not right away, that yes, he has a problem, and yes, he needs help. Whether he decides, after going home, that his real problem is his drinking or his wife will be anyone's guess until he leaves one for the other for good.

After Group I head to the staff room to re-record my chart entries on separate sheets for each client and to do my day's filing. There are two other counsellors and a nurse, all older than me by at least fifteen years, sitting in the overstuffed staff room. No one is talking to each other. It's something I've noticed not only in the Centre but in town—no one here says anything extraneous. It's like words are a limited resource and using too many would be a waste, like paying too much for gas or sending transfer payments to Ottawa. After an hour at the wooden table by the fridge, I finish my work. On the way to Reception I stop by the nurses' station to drop off notes for the night nurse about a few of my clients.

Afterward, I swipe my ID through the slot by the giant double doors leading to Reception. I hear the heavy click that tells me the doors have unlocked, and I push them open heavily with both hands.

A tall, black man in an expensive, brown suede jacket is leaning over the reception desk and talking in fierce, low tones to Carrie, the day host. I know who he is, and I immediately look around the reception area for the two scrawny henchmen whose job it is to calm Gladys's husband down or throw him out.

The first time he showed up, last week, he beat on the security door after slipping by the guards. Carrie said he was yelling Gladys's name over and over, as if she was just on the other side of the door and choosing not to see him. Carrie called the cops to take him away.

I see now that "slipping by security" was probably an exaggeration, since Hank and Gerry are still nowhere to be seen and Carrie's starting to look a bit frantic, although she's doing her best to talk to him reasonably.

The second time, just a few days ago now, Gladys's husband, I think his name is David, left after Hank and Gerry threatened to call the cops again. Carrie said that time he was crying. "Just ask her why from me," he implored her.

He's a big man with dark brown skin, but I can see there are tears cresting his cheekbones. A buzzer starts going off somewhere above me. In the moment before I realize I've been holding the security doors open too long, Gladys's husband looks toward me and the open doors. He runs in my direction. I grab the heavy, metal door handles behind me, one in each hand, and yank them forward as hard as I can. I thud full-body into the charging intruder at the same time I hear the locks click shut.

David's eyes are big and round and project a world of confusion and dismay. The path of tears has dried on each cheek, ending somewhere under his jaw. He's looking down at me like he's shocked to see me.

He sniffles but looks dignified from his height. "I just want to talk to her," he says. His voice is low, his eyes pleading. He's begging me. I take my hands from the door handles and step aside to put some distance between us and to regain my professional composure.

"You should know we aren't allowing Ms. Leroy to see guests at this point in her treatment, Mr.—"

"Blake. David Blake." He seems solemn, professional. For a moment it feels like we're just two professionals introducing ourselves. Then he seems to remember something. "She kept her maiden name," he finishes abruptly.

He's not what I would have expected. His black, leather shoes are polished, his dark dress pants and blue dress shirt are offset with an attractive yellow tie. I can't remember what he does, but it's obvious that wherever Gladys went wrong, she probably didn't take him with her. If you saw him on the street you'd never guess in a million years that his wife was a crack addict, that his children had been taken from their mother, that his newborn was a crack baby. I should know better than to make guesses about people by appearance. Still, sometimes it really is all you have to work with.

"Can I walk with you, Mr. Blake?" I ask, gesturing to the front doors. He gives the security door behind me one last, longing look, and then nods his okay to me. From the corner of my eye, I can see Hank and Gerry arriving from the break room across the reception area as we leave through the front doors.

The wind blows a fine spray of sand from the parking lot into our faces as we come out. We walk down the gravel path, past the hip-high tangle of dying shrubs, and turn right into the lot.

"You're one of her counsellors?" he asks.

"Yes." We're heading toward my car, an aged red Mazda that breaks down every four months. Beyond it is a big, shiny-black SUV.

"Look," he says, stopping. He sets his large, left hand on my shoulder. It's an unexpected motion, and I shrink under the weight. Nervousness presses at me. "I can't imagine what you think of me after I've come charging in there like an idiot. And more than once, at that."

His tone is soft, disarming, his eyes sad.

"And I can only imagine what she's been saying about me... although my guess is not much. She never was one for conversation." A grin edges the corner of his mouth slightly upward, and I can't help smiling, too. Gladys's silence has been a weight in the centre of every one of my days since she arrived. It's reassuring that she was the quiet type in her life before, too.

"Look, Mr. Blake... David, if I may," I say.

He nods a curt yes. His hand is gone from my shoulder, but I can't recall when he did this.

"I can see how hard this must be on you." I catch myself before automatically adding "and your family."

"But we have an excellent program here to help friends and family members cope with their loved one's addictions."

He looks disappointed.

I keep on. "If you'd rather have contact information for any of our counselling counterparts in Calgary, or for an individual therapist, I'd be happy to..." but I've lost him. He's walking away toward the big SUV.

I stand still for a moment, the wind pushing against me. I watch him walk around the enormous box to the driver's side, without ever turning his head to me. As he starts the engine, I walk to the front of my car, waiting for him to pull out so I can get in and go home. His windows are tinted. I try to make out the shape of him behind the wheel, but only see my own reflection in the black hood before he turns and drives off.

Lambeca only has 5,000 people. I pass four liquor stores on my drive home down Main and then Laurence Street. I'm not implying anything. Most of the Centre's clients come from the city, or from other towns just as full of booze and wind and dust and pain. Sometimes they even come here from other provinces, so no one back home can figure out they're not on vacation.

I pull in and park in front of the fourth liquor store, in a mini-mall at the south end of town. I go next door to buy a loaf of bread, a roll of paper towel, a chocolate bar, and a litre of milk. I buy a lottery ticket, scratch it at the counter and get a free play. I scratch the second ticket and only get a snide "Good Luck" in the last scratch box. I've always thought it would be more honest if it said, "Screw You. Buy Another."

I bring my paper bag full of groceries to the car and stow it in the passenger seat. The few remaining blocks home, I keep seeing its motion out of the corner of my eye, the paper towel lolling back and forth on top with each turn. When I look forward, it gives me the constant feeling that someone is sitting next to me.

I pull into the short, gravel drive next to the bungalow I've rented on Avalon Street, a barren suburban street with wind-bent cottonwoods and wire-link fences hedging the lawns of tightly trimmed brown grass. Taking the groceries out of my car, I notice my own lawn is covered in tin cans and plastic bottles. The wind must have knocked someone's recycling box over and blown the contents into my lot. I spot a two-litre pop bottle lying against the cement steps to the front door. Closing the car door, I remember my older brother, Mike, letting me watch him make a bottle rocket when we were kids.

"Hey, brat—wanna be my assistant?"

"Sure!" I said, brimming with instant excitement that he wanted to do something—anything—with me. But then I thought for a moment. Maybe it was a trick.

"For what?" I asked, a bit more subdued.

"You'll see. Come on." My brother led me by the hand into the front yard.

It took him weeks to get all the pipes and joints together, mostly from Dad's friends. He'd laid them all out in the yard. I watched as he put the pieces expertly together from a diagram he'd torn out of a magazine.

"Wrench," he said, and I handed him the wrench from the little row of tools on the lawn. I felt important. It was late afternoon by the time he had everything set up for the first launch.

Mike led me to a spot behind the front porch and told me to stand back. I watched as he pumped the bicycle pump as hard and fast as he could and then yelled, "Fire in the hole!"

The bottle exploded straight up into the air with a loud pop, spraying water behind it. Mike gave an excited whoop and ran to the other end of the yard, to where the rocket had arced and hit the ground, rolling.

"Whoohoo!" he yelled, running back to me with it, smile wide and crazy. Still holding the bottle, he lifted me up and spun me around until I was almost crying from laughing so much.

Mike gave me the honoured job of attaching the bottles for each new launch, and we launched what seemed like a thousand bottles that summer. Hugely careful not to spill too much water from the bottles, I would wind them, upside-down, onto the nozzle of the launch pad, then run back to my spot behind the porch as Mike yelled, "Fire in the hole!"

When Mike invited his friends over to see the launcher, I knew I was about to lose my job as his assistant. I sat on the porch and watched as he showed them our rig. Mike made a big show of the setup, checking the equipment, using his radio-announcer voice to tell them in booming detail what everything was for. Then he said, "I will now let my assistant attach the rocket."

He gestured to me to come get the bottle from him. Walking over to take it, I felt like I was about to pop up into the air with pride.

Going inside now, I think of him the way I normally do: a tombstone in a Vancouver cemetery three years ago, the only time I saw it, the dirt still fresh and the lilies on his grave white and crisp as linen.

After stowing away the groceries, I make dinner and eat in front of the TV: canned ravioli, my specialty. My sister Lisa phones. I ask her how she's doing. She's a year younger than me, but she married Kenny during university, and they have three kids. She tells me the kids are all in swimming this year, and that it's been a real hassle getting all of them off to their practices, each at different times. She also tells me the latest about Dad, as usual. They have Sunday dinner with him and Terry almost every week. Last week, he bought another set of new golf clubs, even though Terry, his boyfriend, our stepfather, had asked him not to, since he already had perfectly good ones, and they're trying to save for a trip to Europe. So now they're bickering about that.

Lisa and I laugh the way we always have. We've spoken a lot more since Mike killed himself. She asks me how I'm doing. I tell her the job's not as bad as I had thought it might be, that the town is actually pretty sometimes, in its prairie-town kind of way, and that I feel like I'm making a difference. We don't talk about Mike; we never do.

There's a pause from her end before we say goodbye, and I know what she wants to ask. I also know she won't. Not again. Not now. And maybe not ever. But my heart skips a beat anyway. I can feel a blush race to my cheeks.

"It's okay," I say, doing my best to sound reassuring. "I'm doing fine. Really."

"Good!" she says. "Good." Both goods come out too forced, and we say our goodbyes quickly.

I put the phone down on the coffee table and stay seated on the worn, yellow plaid couch that came with the furnished house. I catch myself clenching and unclenching my right fist. It's an old, nervous habit, but it reminds me of Gladys's constant tugging at her jeans, and I stop.

The rest of the week is no easier, but there are no major events. No visits from David or from any other angry relatives. Very few confiscations. No attacks. Just a few more new patients, and a couple of graduations. Walter has finished the program and gives me a big bear-trap handshake in the hallway on his way to reception to sign out and see his family.

"You've been a huge help," he says, still shaking and shaking my hand and nodding vigorously. I smile and thank him and wish him the best of luck.

"Stick with it," I tell him by way of encouragement. "Remember—we are all responsible for our own actions."

He'll probably be back within a year. Or maybe he won't. I don't know. It often surprises me—who makes it, who doesn't. I've guessed wrong a lot of times. But, mostly, we don't hear much once they leave the Centre. Walter is in it on his own now.

Gladys's previous Individual Counsellor at the Centre was Ken McConnell. On the surface, he seems happy I'm taking an interest in her.

"She's a tough nut," he says, his feet on his desk, but his expression earnest, "as I'm sure you know by now." He's only about 40, which makes him as close to my age as anyone else here.

"You be careful around her," he says. "That kind will break your heart. Then crack your head open after."

"Anything you're looking to know about her, in particular?" he asks.

I can tell by his overly casual tone he's worried I may be trying to show him up with some sort of brilliant new analysis and treatment plan. He's got nothing to worry about.

"Nah, nothing specific," I say. "I've just been... wondering."

"Ah," says Ken, settling more comfortably into his chair, a knowing smile growing across his face. "The eternal question—where did it all go wrong?"

I smile dutifully and leave Ken's office. My next appointment with Gladys is tomorrow afternoon.

The wind has kicked up again, and I have to lean into it to walk to my car. I can feel it blowing hard from the west, pushing against the passenger side for most of the drive home. If the gusts shove at my car any harder they would push it into the opposite lane. In my driveway, the wind blows fine grains of sand into my eyes. I can hear it howling against the windows and banging the eaves the rest of the evening.

We're not supposed to take clients' files home. I've spread Gladys's case history out on the coffee table. I'm sitting on the floor reading it, my back to the couch, when the doorbell rings. The only people to knock on my door since the Welcome Wagon lady brought me a coupon book and an unnecessary map of the town during my first week have been my landlord, Dad and Terry once, and a steady stream of Mormons offering to save my soul.

I get up and go through the kitchen to the front door.

Gladys Leroy was one of six kids, born and raised in Edmonton. She started out as a dancer. She went to the University of Calgary, got good grades, changed majors, and graduated with a B.Sc. in Chemistry. She started working in research and development for one of the city's biggest oil firms. She made lab supervisor within three years. She taught dance at the YMCA on Saturdays. She met David Blake.

The man on my porch isn't here to save me. From behind the screen door, David Blake looks angry. The sun is starting to set behind him, shadowing his features, and the wind is billowing his open leather coat. He is staring at me. I start to say "Can I help you?" but only get as far as "Can—"

"Ms. Reid," he says, as if assigning me my name. I suddenly wonder if he's come to do something to me. Does he blame me for keeping him from his wife? What would he be willing to do to get to her?

"How did you find out where I live?" I ask. Is there anything nearby I could use as a weapon? Maybe the fire extinguisher in the hall closet, or the keys on the entry table.

Unlike his wife, David Blake has no trouble making eye contract. I can't seem to look away and feel I'm quickly losing any ground I held by this being my home.

"I'm sorry," he says, more gently now, soft, warm tones in his voice. "I followed you the other day."

I tell myself to ask him questions, get him talking, diffuse the situation. Pretend it's a violent client. I've been trained for this.

"Why?" I ask. Yes, good girl.

"I wanted to talk to you... about her." He says *her* like he's spitting. I realize I've moved closer to the door to talk to him. I can smell liquor on his breath.

"I don't usually provide family-member counselling, Mr. Blake, but if you phone the Centre I'm sure—"

He slams his left hand hard against the doorframe, then closes his eyes tightly as if he's in pain. The wind is howling around him.

"Dammit," he mutters. "You know," he's staring into my eyes again, "you're the fourth person in the last freaking week that's told me something like that?" His mood settles again. "I don't need more questions," he says. He leans forward, his face moving toward the screen and into the light from the hallway. "All I want is a couple of freaking answers."

His eyes, dark brown and almost too big for their sockets, are wet. He looks worried, lost. Now that I can see him more clearly, he looks more like a confused, overgrown boy than a raging menace of a man.

He sniffles.

"Fuck," he mumbles and looks back down at the doorstep. Whatever you do, I think, do not invite him in.

"I'm sorry," he says again and backs away from the door. He looks so lost.

"Wait!" I call. My hand is on the doorknob. He stops on the porch steps and turns to face me again.

"Do you want to come in?" I ask. I open the screen door for him. Have I gone insane? What the hell am I doing? I can picture myself next week inviting gang members over for dinner.

He doesn't object when I offer to make tea.

I show him to the living room, then realize Gladys's file is strewn everywhere. I walk ahead to the coffee table and gather the papers into their folder, which I carry into the kitchen with me and tuck on top of the fridge.

Gladys Leroy and David Blake were married a month after her 27th birthday. He was a broker's assistant. Now he's the head of his own mortgage-brokering firm, one of the fastest growing in western Canada. As mortgage brokers go, he's a pretty big shot, according to Gladys's description from one of her first treatment visits.

Ten months after their wedding, Gladys took maternity leave. She never went back. In eight years she went from chemist and lab supervisor to full-time mom to crack addict, having five kids in between, the second-last stillborn. It was after her first she started slipping. For a long time it was prescription drugs, barbiturates with alcohol. Later it was heroin, cocaine. After the stillborn it became crack.

The pattern's not hard to identify, but what bothers me is how she got so far from her starting point. No, that's not true. I've seen lots of people do it. What I really want to know is how she sank so far in isolation. For all his anguish, David Blake is sitting on my couch, is still the head of his firm, is still... not like *her.*

I bring David his tea. Before I can sit down, he starts. "Do you know yet... Has she… Have you ever figured out why she does it? Why she destroys herself?"

He looks earnest, pleading. He's not sure what he did to cause this, when he did it.

"I don't know what they've told you," he adds, "but I never hurt her. Never. I could never have."

I sit down at the other end of the couch.

"I honestly can't say what triggered things for your wife." I take a deep breath and sigh. "She's... tough to reach." I'm not allowed to tell him anything about her case. And what I could tell wouldn't help him anyway.

"She's an addict," I say. "It's a disease. There would have been very little anyone else could have done to stop her from taking this path once she got herself on it. For many people, it's how they respond to stress, how they come to deal with emotion, with reality."

I lean forward. I am not saying exactly what I've been trained to say. But it's what he needs to hear.

"All I can tell you is I'm sure it wasn't anything you did, anything you said, anything specific at all that first set her off, or that brought her to this point. Biologically, genetically, it was probably inevitable no matter what happened in her life."

David stares into his tea. I can't see his face, but his shoulders have relaxed. Maybe I've finally taken some of the weight away. I hope I have.

Eventually he slowly puts the mug down on the coffee table. He gets up.

"Thank you," he says. "I don't know if what you've told me is the truth or not. But thank you."

I just nod. I feel like anything else I could say now would be redundant, or sound stupid.

I see him to the door. On the front porch he turns and looks intently into my eyes again. Maybe he's still searching for one last answer. The wind has finally calmed to a breeze, and I can hear the beetles and the grasshoppers on the lawns all around.

"Remember, no one can help her," I say by way of goodbye, "unless or until she wants us to."

David nods his understanding. He walks away toward the intersection. As he crosses through and keeps walking, I wonder how far away he parked. I have a feeling he didn't do whatever he came to do. Or maybe he did. I don't know.

I close the door.

The night Dad called about Mike, I hadn't seen my brother in nearly two years. Even then, he had already fallen a long way from being the promising young artist painting his way toward an honours B.F.A.

The last time I had gone home to Vancouver for Christmas, I caught him shooting up in the bathroom. Everyone knew he was into something bad, but I was shocked to see him shaking at the airport. I had already finished my psychology degree, and had started in a master's counselling program. As soon as we were alone, I started to tell him everything he should do to get better; I told him what his options were, how to get help, that I would be there for him.

"Mind your own fucking business," he said, slamming the bathroom door with his foot.

He was taking after Mom, and I couldn't stand it. She had left Dad five years before, after he came out of the closet. He had always propped her up. Now she was living on welfare and booze in a rented apartment in Edmonton with the latest in a long line of loser, windbag drinking buddies. I don't know how she got the money to get to Vancouver that Christmas. I guessed it was Dad, but he wouldn't say.

Once we all sat down to dinner, I announced what I had caught Mike doing. I told everyone I thought he had a serious problem, that we should all try to help him through it. Mike swore at me before I could finish, flung his napkin at my face and stalked out to the backyard. Terry seemed shocked. Lisa was furious at Mike and raged out after him. Dad stayed quiet. I realized he must have known for some time what had been happening.

Mom sided with Mike. She told me I should mind my own business.

"You think you're so goddamn high and mighty, don't you?" she spat at me. "I don't know where the hell you came from. I never would have raised a little bitch like you."

She was the only one to keep eating. I didn't see her, or Mike, again until the funeral.

I would swear the entire staff, starting with the front receptionist and security, have been looking at me strangely since I got in this morning. It's like they all want to tell me something, but then decide not to. It's a busy day , though, and I don't have time for their problems on top of everyone else's.

There are two newcomers in Group—Steve and Laura. They're both still shaky from withdrawal and the D.T.s, respectively. It's a quiet group. Even Gladys is still.

I spend my afternoon break, as usual, doing paperwork in the psychiatric-staff room. When I'm done with my notes, I notice there is a copy of today's *Calgary Sun* under my stack of folders. I pull it out and flip through it, glossing along the headlines. There's a familiar face in a profile picture on page eight. It's under the heading "Dad of 5 Drives off Bridge after Losing Family."

Driving home, my hands feel numb and weightless on the steering wheel. I realize my heart has been racing; I don't know for how long. I picture myself getting home. I see myself tearing through the house with a garbage bag, loading it with the bottle of Scotch whisky from the cupboard, the gin under the nightstand, the other whisky in the hall closet, tucked behind the fire extinguisher. I picture myself hauling the bag to a far-off dumpster that I will also, ridiculously, hope the other me—the one that wants to drink them all right now, in quick succession, until the world goes away, until I go away— won't remember how to get to.

When I get home, I lock the screen door behind me. I close the wooden door after it, turn the deadbolt into place. I hold onto it for a minute. I could leave. I could... I head for the kitchen. I find the whisky I hid from myself behind the dish soap, under the sink. I put it on the counter and draw a glass tumbler from a different cupboard.

The bottle, the glass, and I go back to the couch in the living room. I try not to. I try not to. And then I pour. I suck the sweet and bitter heat in in a long and single draught that warms my heart and my fingertips and soothes my brain with angry, guilted bliss. The glass looks so lonely with just the swirl of brassy syrup left lingering at the base. So I refill it.

"Don't worry," I tell the whisky. "I'm fine. Everyone is fine."

Starting

"And so Napi took the mud and formed it into a woman and a boy, and he said to them 'You must be people.'"—Blackfoot legend, Head-Smashed-In Buffalo Jump

Napi rolls clay from the river basin in his god-hands and mixes it to smooth ochre. Maybe he rests. Trickster, shape-shifter, sitting on the cliff of the gorge, water's slippery edge, vision set on the mud rivers unflowing in his palm. Is there a plan at the ledge of beginnings? An image the raven carried here in his thoughts, figure of flesh, to be formed from the earth and the wet, the residue of decay and rain?

Before the sun there was the air and the dark sailing of the powerful crow, plucking the bright eye of the universe and hanging it high to look over his creations. Napi's fortune at the dawn is to be a mixed history of allegory passed from one tribe to the next, but always the creator's, told with different names, implications.

Napi sits by the river and thinks it is good. He will make his people tall and upright, standing free in the foothills, able to roam the mountains and the plains: fishers and hunters, barterers and dancers, singers of dreams and shapers of worlds beyond this. Their agile hands will build much.

Napi sees they have already grown beyond him—this woman, this boy. He does not know what they will build, cannot foresee them once they leave the river's bed. This, he knows, may prove to be a problem. But he will set them in motion, regardless. He will tell them what they are and leave the rest to them.

Calamity Sam

Calamity Sam tumbles into the room, smitten and be-gloved, moaning the virtues of a true teenage god. Adam. What a name. The first man.

He's not a man yet, of course, just a boy, but Sam could help with that. Maybe. Given the chance. Not that Sam's like that. Forward, unvirtuous. No. But, still, given opportunity... just imagine.

Adam is new in town. February has blown him in, friendly and warm, in place of a chinook, gusted him onto the prairie with the drifting tumbleweed. Straight into Sam's English class. And French. Wow. Adam smiles a lot. Adam smiled right at Sam first. Before even looking at anyone else.

Adam comes from Markham, Ontario. That's practically Toronto. He must have gone there all the time. Sam would have, but Sam never even gets to go to Calgary, unless they're picking someone up from the airport. Boring.

Sam's mom gets to hear all about Adam at dinner. Adam is tall. And Adam must be rich, not that that's important, but his parents bought the motel at the corner of Waterton and Main, and they must be rich to do something like that, and Adam dresses really nicely. Nothing flashy, but everything's labels.

Sam's Dad is in the States on business. Sam's Dad is away a lot, but that's okay, because they have a lot of fun when he's around. Last month they went ice sailing, which was awesome, just crazy fast and Sam got to steer for a while. It was wild.

Sam heads to the 7-11 after dinner to meet Tina and Brie. They already have their Slurpies. Sam goes in to get one and runs into Dan and Laurie buying a massive grape-strawberry to share.

"We could go to the Twilight Inn," Sam says back in the parking lot. "Welcome the new guy." Everyone nods or grumbles agreement. Tina shoots Sam a look. She can tell what Sam's up to. Sam blushes a bit but works some gumption back up. Eyes on the prize, as Sam's Dad says, eyes on the prize.

"We could all go to my place after. My Dad's away, and we could watch old SNLs on the big screen in the basement," says Sam.

Sam gets Laurie to ring the doorbell at the motel. The blinds are open, and Sam can see through the office window to one side of the door. There's a living room piled high with boxes to the other side. An old man opens the door. Adam's grandparents must be helping with the move, or Adam's parents are really old.

"Hello sir. I'm Laurie and these are my friends. Is Adam home, by any chance?" asks Laurie. The man's bushy white eyebrows furrow together like mating caterpillars. Maybe he's deaf. Louder, Laurie adds, "We're from his school. We wanted to welcome him to town, please, if that's okay."

Sam chose well. Laurie's so polite she'd thank you for shoving her out of a speeding truck. It goes over like free money with parents, though, and the man heads off to fetch Adam from deep inside the bungalow.

Back at Sam's, everyone has their snacks. They ran into Jeff and Mark on the way back, and the two are shooting pool with Laurie and Dan. Adam's sitting on the sectional, Tina and Brie sprawled at different angles to either side, chucking popcorn at each other across the new guy.

"Thanks for inviting me," Adam says to Sam.

Sam's tried to stay quiet, keep it to the background, while Adam absorbs that this is Sam's crew, that these are the most popular kids in their school, that Sam's at the centre of it all.

Sam senses Adam is an alpha male. Sam likes psychology—has read that alphas either hang with other leaders, or surround themselves with followers. Sam is definitely not weaker than Adam. It wouldn't work out if Adam went for that, so Adam may as well know now where things are at. That way he can make an informed decision.

"No problem," says Sam. "I figured it can't be easy, being new in town."

Jeff and Mark co-captain the basketball team. Right now they're pretending to beat each other up on top of the pool table. Sam looks over at them and says, "Plus, I figured if anyone was going to introduce you to Willow Creek society, who better than our greatest minds?"

Adam laughs. His voice is warm, delicious to the ears. Sam could just eat that up. Yu-um.

"You've got good friends," says Adam. "That's not easy to come by."

"Hear that, Sam?" says Brie. She's up off the couch, flipping through a tall stack of burned DVDs. "You should love us. And appreciate us."

"And feed us!" calls Tina from the couch. She pops up and heads for the stairs. "More popcorn, anyone?"

Jeff and Mark stop their battle to head up with Tina in search of the unopened bag of guacamole chips they left last week. Laurie and Dan take their shot during the action and quietly slip into one of the rooms down the hall.

"Well, they're not much," says Sam, "but they're mine."

"We love you, too," says Brie. She bounces up the stairs after the rest. "Bathroom break!"

There's a bathroom downstairs, too. Sam's heart suddenly swells with appreciation for everyone in the house. They may be goofy sometimes. But they're definitely not dumb.

There's a long silence between Sam and Adam. Sam has been standing by the TV. Would it be too obvious to move to the couch?

"So, tell me about yourself," Sam says instead of deciding.

"Not much to tell. Just what I told in English. I'm from Markham, I play soccer, my mom's Irish, my dad worked for an ad firm and then they decided to abandon ship and buy a motel."

"Did you have to leave anyone behind?" Sam sits down at the far end of the couch. Better not to push things right away.

"Just my dog, Fred," says Adam. "He was too old to make the trip, so my parents left him with my cousins in the country."

Okay. That was unhelpful.

"Did you have a... you know, girlfriend or anything?"

Adam's face turns sunset pink, and he looks down at the shag carpet. He's grinning, though. "Um, kind of like an 'or anything.' But we broke up way before I left."

Great. He's being cute. Still, broken up is good. What to try next...

"An or anything?"

Adam spreads his arms out across the back of the couch, so his hand is only about a foot from Sam's shoulder. He tilts his head to the right. Puppy dog cute.

"Can I ask you something, Sam?"

"Sure." Sam's heart feels like it's about to pummel its way out.

"Why am I here?"

Sam answers with a smile set, hopefully, for dazzle, says, "You're here because I'm really friendly."

Adam's own smile is off the dazzle-meter. Sam's heart does a full-on break dance. This could totally work.

For forty minutes more they talk about life stuff, where they were born, their roster of exes. Sam's list pretty much totals to minus one, but Adam has only had two real relationships, and one was only for a week, so Sam doesn't feel too bad. Plus, Willow Creek is pretty small, so what can you do?

By the time Sam's friends slink back downstairs, Sam and Adam are sitting side by side on the sofa.

"Hey, Sam. Hey, Adam. Awesome night out," says Tina.

"Yeah, we went to shoot hoops out back," says Mark.

"Yeah, you should have come!" calls Jeff as he bounds down the stairs two at a time. When he gets to the bottom, Brie pokes him in the ribs with an elbow. "What? What'd I say?" says Jeff, protecting himself from further damage by crossing his arms over his stomach.

Laurie and Dan have somehow managed to regroup with everyone, too.

I have the world's most awesome friends ever, thinks Sam, but says "Cool! Glad you had fun."

"Anyway, Dan and I thought we'd get going," says Laurie. "There's baseball tomorrow."

"Yeah, us too," says Tina for her and Brie. They live two doors apart and most people think they must be sisters.

"Yeah, I've got to bail too, man," Jeff says to Sam.

"Me too," adds Mark.

Sam and Adam get up and follow the momentum up the stairs to the front door.

"You need a ride, Adam?" asks Mark.

"Yeah, sure, I'd appreciate that," he answers.

With everyone else already on the porch or in the drive, Adam hangs back by the door. "Just one question," he says to Sam. "Well, two, actually."

"Sure," says Sam, standing inside the doorway. Adam is holding the screen door open from outside.

"Okay. One, when can I see you again?"

"Um. Are you free tomorrow night?"

"Absolutely."

"Cool. Here, around eight?"

"Sure." Big smile from Adam. *Wow. Oh, shut up, heart*, Sam thinks past the pounding.

"And your other question?" Sam asks, taking the door from Adam and stepping out slightly onto the porch.

Adam leans in. "Are your friends totally cool?"

Anita Dolman

Sam looks over Adam's shoulder. Jeff and Mark are waiting in Jeff's pick-up, arguing over what music to play on the two-minute drive to Adam's. Tina and Brie are standing in the drive, looking at Brie's iPod. Dan and Laurie are on the porch steps, Dan helping Laurie into her coat. A gentleman. Sam knows what Adam is asking. A big car rounds the corner, stage-lighting everyone like it's a moment in a play.

"Yeah, they're totally cool."

"Good." Adam kisses Sam square on the lips.

"Aw, man!" calls Mark from the truck. "I do not need to see that." Brie and Tina applaud and cat call from the driveway. Laurie shouts, "Good work, Sam!" Dan laughs and says "Hey! Get a room already!"

Sam can feel his and Adam's lips curl into smiles, but they keep the kiss going.

The car coming around the corner stops dead in front of the house with a deep, loud squeal. Sam and Adam break away to look as Sam's Dad rolls their silver SUV slowly the last few feet up the drive. Tina and Brie scatter quickly onto the lawn.

"Fuck," Dan says, the sudden gravity of what's happening not lost on him or on anyone else in the crowd. He and Laurie turn to Sam, whose formerly bounding heart has plummeted into his shoes. "You want us to stay a bit?" Dan asks Sam.

Adam has pulled back and is looking from the SUV to Sam. "Your dad?" he asks as the driver's door opens.

"Yeah," says Sam, watching his Dad all the while. "You'd better go."

Adam looks worried for Sam, reaches his hand toward Sam's as if to squeeze, but catches himself, pulls back right away.

"You sure?"

"Yeah. Go."

Sam's dad walks ultraslow. Everyone is still watching. Except for Sam, they all look braced, ready to leap to his aid if he needs it. Adam moves to the porch rail to let the broad, balding man in the business suit pass. The man ignores him, is trained directly on Sam and only Sam. He looks a kind of angry that Adam has only seen in movies.

"Sam." The man's voice sounds like he's trying very hard not to yell, to sound reasonable in front of other human beings.

"Dad." Sam takes a step back.

"Inside."

Jeff and Mark stay in the truck with Adam for a few minutes, but it's impossible to tell what's going on in the house. If Sam's Dad is yelling at him, it must be downstairs, because they can't hear anything from the street, so Mark starts the truck to take Adam home.

"Just how much shit did I get Sam in, do you think?" asks Adam from the back seat of the extended cab.

"It ain't you, man," says Mark. "This has been coming for a while. Man's a fuckhead. Doesn't even try to figure Sam out."

"Seriously," says Jeff. "He wouldn't have had a clue Sam was gay. I mean, it's Sam. Like, no offense, but there's queer and then there's *queer*, and Sam has always been pretty fucking queer. Like, how could the guy seriously not know?"

"Does the whole school know Sam's gay?" asks Adam.

"Yeah, sure, I guess," says Jeff. "I mean anyone that knows him. Like I said, it'd be hard not to catch on. He used to have a poster of Adam Lambert in his locker, and he doesn't exactly act like other guys. Plus he's totally out of the closet with all of his actual friends."

"But he's, like, the most popular kid in school?"

"I'd say so," says Mark. "I mean, other than me, of course."

"Huh." Adam is mulling it over, still can't reconcile the two tough, small-town Albertans in the front seat as being best friends with a known fag.

"No offense, guys, but you know, I'd kind of thought moving here would be a little more, I mean, except for Sam's Dad, I would have thought it would be more, you know, overall…"

"Redneck?" asks Mark. "It is. It's still total backwater shit in a lot of ways. I mean, it's amazing they don't burn a stake on the lawn of any house with a Green Party sign at election time. But I've been thinking about it lately, and the thing is, in a town this small, in a school this small, I think there's just not enough population to fill all the roles separately. Laurie's a cheerleader but she's got CP. The mayor's a former crackhead. And I'm co-captain of the basketball team, but anywhere else I'd probably just be a total geek. I even have my own workshop. I've won at the regional science fair two years running. Went to provincials. But you just don't have room to segregate here. So all the freaks have to step up."

Jeff has been nodding at Mark's entire speech. They've clearly discussed the strange idiosyncrasies of Willow Creek culture before.

"Yeah," he says. "It's weird that way, but it's kind of a cool thing about small towns. Everyone's a freak, and everyone knows it, which also means nearly everyone has a shot at being some kind of cool."

Calamity Sam is lying in bed, machine beeping slowly, bright sunshine pouring in through the window.

Sam's mom is at the bedside, where she's been since last night.

"Oh, Calamity Sam," she says softly. "What a thing for you to do."

Sam wakes and he sees his mom crying. "Hey. Hey, Mom," he says. "Hey, it's alright."

Sam looks around him at the little hospital room, with its little TV sitting dark, high up in the corner between peeling yellow walls.

Sam is being gently hugged through the sheets by his mom, who is still crying. Sam hugs back feebly, is suddenly aware of just how sore and stiff he is. Everything hurts, and his left hand and wrist are in a cast. The right side of his face feels bulged and tight. It must be swollen.

"Whoa, Mom, cut it out. It's okay. But you're going to knock me out again if you keep squeezing."

"Sorry, honey," she says sitting back down in the little straight-backed chair by the bed. She keeps hold of Sam's hand. She gathers herself together, earnest, takes a deep breath.

"I have to know, though, honey, why did you do it? What could he possibly have said to you to make you do such a thing?" She leans forward, expectant. "You know everyone loves you. Your friends love you. I love you. And your father does, too. He never should have reacted the way he did, but he never wanted to hear..."

She bites her bottom lip a moment before going on.

"He never should have said what he said," she continues. "He's so smart in a lot of ways, but he can't process things like other people sometimes. But you, you can't take it so personally. Your father's a bit of an idiot, sweetheart. He needs time sometimes. It doesn't mean he doesn't love you."

Sam's brain feels squishy. There's something wrong behind all the nice things his mom just said. Sam remembers his Dad losing it after seeing Sam and Adam kissing on the porch. Sam thinks of the kiss instead of the argument. He can't help but smile and feels a slicing pain. He realizes his lip is cut. Something else happened. *Oh, shit.*

"Mom, no. No. No, no, no, no, no." Sam tries to shake his head to express just how very no what's she's thinking is. "Mom, no, I totally did not try to kill myself. Oh, my God. No." Sam's mom looks baffled. And Sam knows what he's saying isn't, strictly speaking, one-hundred per cent totally true, but he certainly didn't do it like she must think he did.

"Sweetheart," Sam's mom says slowly, as if Sam isn't all there, and she's filled with pity to find this out, "they found you at the bottom of the coulee. You jumped off the railway bridge."

Sam's dad had pointed downstairs to the rec room once they got inside. Sam could sense his friends waiting outside to see what would happen next. His mom had gone to bed ages ago, while everyone was still there. She must not have known either that Sam's dad was coming.

Sam's dad sat down on the sectional. Sam sat, too, since staying standing would have been even more awkward. Sam thought of how much angrier his dad would be if he knew Adam had been sitting there earlier, flirting with his son, talking about past boyfriends, or the lack thereof, about all the things that would make two people decide if they wanted to date.

Sam's heart was racing in a completely different way, now. There was a lot of silence before his dad looked up from his folded hands and said, "I guess I'm probably the last person to find out you're a fucking faggot, huh?"

Things didn't get better from there, but Sam didn't really stand up for himself, either, now that he thinks of it. He let his dad tell him how embarrassed he was, how it was Sam's fault his dad wouldn't be able to show his face at the Kiwanis Hall anymore, would never have grand kids. Sam sat and took it while his dad called him disgusting, told him society had gone too far letting queers marry, asked how God could have given him a son who'd never be a man. He was talking to himself more than to Sam by then.

Then he said something Sam couldn't absorb.

"If I'd known your mother was going to give me a faggot, I never would have married her," he said. He was looking Sam right in the eye, and Sam was crying. "I should have known this would happen. You've always been such a disappointment. I give up. You're not my son anymore."

Then Sam's dad got up, went up the stairs, walked out the front door, and drove away.

Sam sat for a long time, watching the stairs. Then he got up, took a full bottle of rum from the liquor cabinet, and headed out the front door, too.

Sam drank in the park until the world went wobbly and almost every wrong in the world could be blamed on his dad, or at least on men like him.

The next thing he remembered, he'd walked into the Alberta Saloon.

Sam had never been inside the dim and dingy bar before, but it was pretty much how he'd always pictured it. Dimly little. A long, wooden bar. Budweiser and Blue posters. Sticky floors. The smell of beer and leather and wet wood, and probably three kinds of mold.

Sam thought he'd get carded and kicked out as soon as he walked in, since he was entirely aware that he looked like a queer, blonde, preppy seventeen-year-old and nothing else.

But he didn't. The bar was almost empty, except for two drug dealers playing pool in the back, a couple of cowboys at the bar, a very tired-looking, pregnant waitress refilling ketchup bottles, and a tall, female bartender with long, black hair. She was wearing a faux-country, lacy, white blouse. It was open so low, Sam thought she must be trying to give free anatomy lessons. She looked right at Sam as he sat at the bar, but she didn't say or offer a thing, just kept on drying the pint glasses and lining them on the rear counter in front of a giant mirror. Sam wondered why anyone would want to watch themselves drink. Especially here. After all, if you were drinking here, you probably didn't want to see what was about to happen to you next.

Jason Rundell sat down on the stool next to Sam. He'd been sitting at the far end of the bar, but Sam hadn't noticed anything more about the person sitting there than that he was male and old and wearing a Stetson. A real one. Jason Rundell had been an actual cowboy once. In the rodeo. He knew Sam's dad. Sam forgot how exactly. Sam had always said hello to Mr. Rundell whenever he saw him in town. Mr. Rundell backed a lot of community events, and of course, the local rodeo. Sam wasn't sure what he actually did, though, or how he got the money to back so many things. Maybe he had a ranch. Maybe he'd gotten rich in the rodeo.

"Bit young still for the saloon, ain't you, son?" asked Mr. Rundell. "Unless I got your age wrong, of course. Everyone's growin' so damned quick these days."

And that easily, all the nerve washed out of Sam. Mr. Rundell was being kind, giving him the option of a lie or an excuse. Sam had expected much worse in coming here, to be honest. Now that it looked like he hadn't found it, he felt uncertain and, for the first time since he'd walked in, a bit scared.

"No," said Sam. "You're not wrong." He looked down at the oak bar. A peeled Bud label had turned to mush in a puddle of beer or condensation in the spot where a beer would have been right now if Sam had been older.

Mr. Rundell stayed quiet for a long while. He seemed to be thinking.

"It's not my place, I suppose, to be giving you advice," he said. He paused, leaving Sam room to agree if he'd rather not get any.

Sam didn't. But he didn't have high hopes for whatever advice Mr. Rundell might have.

"I'm gonna take me a guess that you run into some trouble with that father of yours," said Mr. Rundell. "And I'm gonna take me another guess that you got your heart, and maybe even your marching papers, handed you."

Sam had never considered his dad might kick him out. He was there so much more than his dad; it foolishly hadn't occurred to him that was a possibility. Somehow, he'd been completely sure his mom would never let something like that happen. But Sam's heart sank even deeper, wondering which of them she would really have chosen if it had come to it. After all, Sam's dad was her husband. They'd been married almost twenty years.

"No. I've still got a home," Sam told Mr. Rundell. "At least, far as I know."

"Well, that's something, then," said the old cowboy. He pushed his hat back, and Sam noticed there was still quite a bit of blonde among his grey hairs. Mr. Rundell's face, though, was weathered with years of sun. Tanned and tough, it was wrinkled as linen.

"My dad walked out, though."

"Found out you was queer?"

Sam paused for a second before answering. "Yeah," he said. He looked Mr. Rundell in the eye for the first time, looked at him questioningly. How did he know? Sam had thought of him as living and thinking in the 1880s.

Mr. Rundell looked away, took a swig of the beer he'd brought over.

"No offense, son, but your dad ain't too bright regardin' people, is he?" he asked Sam in the mirror.

Sam stared at Mr. Rundell's reflection for a moment. Laughter started to bubble inside him. It spilled out abruptly, loud and hard. The laughter fed itself as Sam laughed toward the mirror, toward his own reflection, and then at Mr. Rundell himself. He could hear the sound of it outside him, echoing through the bar.

Even ancient Mr. Rundell had known, probably since Sam was a kid, that Sam was queer. And he was a tough, old rodeo cowboy who only saw Sam a couple of times a year. Even him. But not his own dad. Sam laughed and laughed. The old man smiled at him sweetly, like a grandfather at a giggle-delirious toddler, waiting patiently for Sam to calm down.

"You suppose," Sam said as his laughter finally slowed, "there's anyone else who's ever met me, anyone else in the whole town, even, who didn't know?"

Mr. Rundell looked like he was really considering that, then, nodding agreement to his own answer, said, "Well, I think I'd have to probably go with 'No,' son. Not anyone what's met you." And then he laughed, too.

Mr. Rundell told Sam he was going to have to get him out of the bar, although it was alright if Sam didn't want to head home just yet, so they headed to the parking lot. Sam asked to be dropped off at the park by the old railway bridge, a half dozen blocks from his house.

As Sam got out of the pickup, Mr. Rundell said, "Sam. I never did give you that advice. I hope you don't mind taking it."

Sam looked up into the cab. Mr. Rundell took his hat off and laid it in his lap.

"You're a good kid, Sam. Always have been, far as I know. And what you need to do is not listen to that asshole father of yours. Pardon me. But Willow Creek don't produce much of note, and I'll tell you, there ain't no one what's ever met you thought you weren't queer. But there also ain't no one that I ever heard met you that thought you weren't gonna do somethin' big with your life. People can tell a thing like that." He looked thoughtful again. "Well, most people can."

He gave Sam a single, serious nod to show he was done with his advice.

"Thanks," said Sam and closed the door. He saw Mr. Rundell tap his hat back on before he drove off.

Sam wandered through the park, thinking. Ever since Adam had kissed him, Sam had been trying to hold onto that awesome part of the night. He knew he'd have to let go of the lousy part to really do it, but he thought he'd give himself one good wallow before he tried to let it go.

Sam remembers opening the little bottle of rum again, deciding to climb out on the decommissioned railway trestle, like he and Tina and Mark used to do when they were kids. He would just sit for a while, let the town sleep and dream and putter its way through the night below.

Then Sam woke up to see his mother crying in his hospital room.

Calamity Sam is asleep when Adam comes in with a bunch of flowers. Adam waits until Sam wakes up.

"Oh, shit," Sam says when he wakes to see him.

"Hello to you, too," answers Adam with a grin.

"What are you doing here?" asks Sam.

"I came for our date."

Sam groans. He wants to die from embarrassment. No—not die. He didn't mean that. Just disappear until Adam comes to his senses and leaves.

"I am the world's biggest idiot," says Sam.

"No," says Adam. "You're just a giant drama queen. When Jeff and Mark told me you were here, I thought your Dad had beaten you up."

"Just emotionally." Sam spots the flowers on the side table, bright yellows and oranges with a burgundy Gerber daisy. "Thanks for those."

"Well, like I said, it is a date," Adam says with a wink.

"Oh, don't do that," says Sam. "I'm not sure my heart can take it right now."

"When do they let you out?" asks Adam, taking the chair by the bed.

"Tomorrow. Assuming they think I'm not going to try and kill myself again," says Sam. "Which I didn't! Try I mean," he adds quickly, sitting up as much as he can. "You heard that, right?"

"Yeah, it came across the wires. Your mom and Tina have been keeping everyone updated. At least, once they realized you didn't try to throw yourself off a bridge. Either way, I'm grateful you weren't hurt more," says Adam. He puts his feet up on the metal edge of the bed. "Mind?"

"Nope."

"And your Dad?"

"He hasn't come. Mom said he went back to California. He'd taken a break to surprise us for the weekend. I don't think Mom's very happy with him right now."

"Well, I hope you don't take this the wrong way, Sam, but I kind of hope your Dad stays the hell away if this is how he treats you."

Adam puts his feet back on the floor and leans forward toward Sam.

"So you don't think I'm the biggest freak ever?"

Adam kisses Sam on the lips, then leans his forehead against Sam's.

"Totally not. And, anyway, from what I've heard, being a freak will get you pretty far in this town."

About the Author

Anita Dolman's poetry and fiction have been published throughout Canada and the United States, including in *Matrix Magazine, Triangulation: Lost Voices, Grain, The Antigonish Review, On Spec, Geist and PRISM international.* She is the author of two poetry chapbooks, *Where No One Can See You* (AngelHousePress, 2014) and *Scalpel, Tea and Shotglass* (above/ground press, 2004), and is a contributing editor for *Arc Poetry Magazine.* She lives in Ottawa, on unceded Algonquin territory, with her partner, child, and cat.

Blog: http://anitadolman.blogspot.ca/
Twitter: @ajdolman

CPSIA information can be obtained
at www.ICGtesting.com
Printed in the USA
LVOW10s1935280417
532583LV00014B/153/P